Dedicated to Beckie, my girls and all my family (including the hounds).

Warning: This book contains offensive language.

Harold's Price

Paul Ravenscroft

Stepney, 1951

It's been raining, and the concrete is slick.

I'm perched on the edge of the coal bunker in the back yard of our house, watching my brothers kick a knackered brown football around. We're all out this warm early summer evening, even Edward who's off to join the army when he turns eighteen in a few weeks' time. He's my idol and the family are all proud of him.

There's not much in our yard. Just the bunker, an outside loo and the concrete walls and floor. A battered wooden ladder lies useless underneath the back window and the only greenery, the weeds that creep through the cracks and round the edge of the house.

Edward's kicking about with Henry, who's older than me by two years and David, younger by three. Then there's me, not long turned eleven, perched here watching and laughing as Edward keeps the ball away from the other two, eventually letting them take it off him and run off to score against the back wall. We're all laughing and enjoying the moment as Henry races round with one hand in the air, thinking he's Harry bloody Hooper.

Mum hears the bang of the heavy leather against the wall and appears at the back door almost in an instant. "Careful you lot. You'll have the neighbours round screaming blue murder".

"Sorry Mum" replies Edward, smiling and hardly out of breath.

"Just see you behave". But now she's smiling too and disappears back into the kitchen.

Edward turns to me. "Come on Harold, get down here and play. We need a midfield general."

I'm all smiles as I jump down off the bunker but the other two aren't laughing. They're looking at Edward and then back at me. They know what might be coming but they're not going to argue with their older brother.

So, we're off again. David keeping his distance, trying to pass it or kick it away as quickly as it comes to him. Not that he's any bloody good. Can't kick straight with his right foot, and that's his best one. His left is barely good enough for standing on.

Henry carries on as before, trying to get the ball and eventually does, making a dash for the back wall. He's shouting something about West Ham and about to blast another goal when I come crashing in, taking his legs and the ball all in one go. We both hit the concrete with a slap, him landing partly on top of me.

By the time Edward's dragged us apart, Henry's got a bloody lip and my shirt is halfway up my back. We're still swearing and throwing punches as he tries to hold us away from each other. Both of us careful not to catch Edward with a stray fist, so the anger gradually ebbs away.

David stands there watching for a moment, then runs inside to do what he does best. Grass us all up.

Edward calls out to him to hang on, but David's already gone, so he quickly tries to straighten us up and wipe the blood away from Henry's fattening lip while we just stare daggers at each other. But it's too little too late. Mum appears again at the back door with a face like thunder. We're all in for it now. Me most of all.

Wednesday 5th March 1969.

"Notorious London gangsters, Ronald and Reginald Kray, were yesterday found guilty of the murders of George Cornell and Jack McVitie. Justice Melford Stevenson said..."

Harold switched off the radio. Like the rest of the country, he'd already read the news in yesterday evening's papers. There wouldn't be anything else worth knowing until later this afternoon when the sentences would be handed down.

Jostling for position began soon after they were arrested last year. The main London gangs had been readying themselves for this day, taking little bits of territory from each other here and there, but no one had made any significant moves in case the twins walked free. Now their reign was over and with most of their firm going down with them or turning grass, the field was well and truly open.

Harold wandered over to the window and stared out from his fifth-floor flat across Stepney towards the river. The window faintly reflected a short, thick set and powerful individual with closely cropped black hair receding a little at the front and thick sideburns. And eyes inherited from his mother that bore right through you.

Harold White was Stepney born and bred. This was his manor. Technically it was George Patterson's manor, but Harold was one of the top lieutenants and an important part of George's organisation.

It was a clear and bright morning, but as he stood there gazing out, Harold preferred the view when it had been raining, as it gave the rooftops and drab streets a shine. Many of the people under those rooftops lived in cramped, crowded conditions and deserved a lot better. The people of East London worked hard or ducked and dived to provide for their families, and even if there wasn't much money about, there was a lot of love.

The flat he shared with Paula wasn't crowded or cramped, or full of love for that matter. They'd wanted something with a balcony but even Harold's money couldn't secure that in time. One day, he told himself, he'd have the balcony and a lot more, perhaps even looking out over the river and maybe a pad up west as well. Harold was conscious he was thinking about what he wanted, rather than what they'd both have one day. It was something Paula often accused him of, particularly during their increasingly regular arguments. They were an ambitious couple, but those ambitions seemed to be moving in separate directions.

On a day like today you could almost see all the way to the river from the flat. Harold wondered what was going through the mind of Alfred Kemble, who ran things down by the river along Wapping and Limehouse. Kemble was old school, like Harold's boss, but had a ruthless streak that Patterson missed, and so consequently had a more lucrative patch and a bigger firm. If they decided they were going to take over in Stepney then Harold and his colleagues had problems, but he wasn't going to go down without a fight.

Harold admired and detested Kemble in equal measure, and knew the latter feeling was mutual. They'd met a few times socially and never got on. He'd marked Harold as a potential threat early on and nothing was going to change his opinion. If there was a war, he knew Kemble would top him the first chance he got. The man was a snake and always plotting and scheming, often involving winding up Patterson or chipping away at his empire. It had only been the twins keeping him at bay all these years.

He'd expected a call from Ray by now and felt disappointed as he needed cheering up, which was something Ray always seemed to manage. Nothing worried Ray who breezed through life looking for a good time, or at least that's how it appeared to everyone who knew him. But Harold knew him better than anyone. Back when they were teenagers doing their national service, Ray had saved his life, and that was something he'd never forget.

He was snapped out of his thoughts by Paula's voice, coming from the bedroom.

"Harold!"

"What?" he shouted back, still looking out of the window.

She came to the doorway. "I'm going shopping then over your mum's. Won't be back 'til this afternoon. You gonna be home for dinner?"

"Doubt it. I've got a busy day. Just do me something and leave it in the oven."

Paula crossed her arms and stared at him from the doorway as he continued looking out of the window. After a short silence she turned away and picked up her things. Harold heard the front door slamming shut.

She'd got the hump again. Surely, she knew he couldn't be home at half past five on the dot like some office worker, with tea on the table and a night in front of the television. That wasn't him, or his life and it never would be.

Another cup of tea seemed like a good idea right now, so he put the kettle on the cooker and turned on the gas, flicking the ignition switch the blue flames shot out from underneath and he had to pull his hand back quickly, turning the gas down to a lower level. He was too heavy handed, in almost everything he did. Sometimes it got you burned.

As he stood in the kitchen waiting for the kettle to boil, Harold thought back to when he'd first met his wife. Back then she was a sparky little brunette and they'd hit it off straight away. In those days she was always up for a laugh, a little stunner full of life who enjoyed a night on the town and appreciated a few quid if he'd had a good earner that week. Marrying a year after they met, they were happy for a while but over the past few years Harold believed she was gradually turning into a watered-down version of his mother.

He knew he was partly to blame, letting his family dominate their life and as a result Paula had grown close to his mum. Now her influence was rubbing off on his wife and he was fucked if he was going to end up like his own father, worn down by the constant nagging.

Although he'd didn't like to admit it, maybe he'd changed over the years as well. When they'd first got together, he was just another member of the gang, running errands and doing a bit of work here and there. Occasionally he'd get involved in an earner and have a bit extra which they often blew straight away. But gradually, over the years he'd become integral to the firm and much more involved in their day-to-day business, which meant being out a lot, often during unsocial hours and going off here and there at the last minute. That seemed to bother her more than anything else.

The phone rang, and the kettle started to whistle at the same time. He took the kettle off the cooker, turned off the gas and went out to the hallway to pick up the phone, glad of the distraction from his thoughts.

"Alright Harold" said a cheery voice on the other end of the line.

"Ray" Harold smiled. "How are ya?"

"I'm alright darlin'. How's yourself?" came the reply. Harold could tell Ray had a cigarette in his mouth, as usual.

"Leave off! It's too early in the morning for all that." he laughed. "We need to talk. You going to the Britannia later?"

"Yeah. See you in there at eleven?"

"See you there."

The line went dead. Harold was still smiling to himself. Just having a few words with his best mate made him feel better and he was looking forward to having a drink with him later. Ray liked having a few whiskies to ease himself into the day and he was probably on his second by now, but it'd never been a problem. Some of the firm took issue with Ray's lifestyle, but they'd take issue whatever he did. The man was like marmite.

Harold went back to the kitchen and turned the radio back on. The news had ended, replaced by The Who. Now that's a proper band, thought Harold. None of this flower power crap. He'd been a bit of a mod back in the early sixties and already started growing out of it by the time The Who came along, but he loved their music and even more so now they were morphing into rock stars. He ditched the thought of tea and opened the cupboard, taking out the whisky bottle. It was going to be a long day and if a little sharpener was good enough for his mate, it was good enough for him.

*

In the well-furnished bedroom of his well-furnished detached house, George Patterson picked out his suit for the day ahead. Radio Three murmured away in the background but he paid it little interest now the news had finished. He usually enjoyed the modern jazz they played in the mornings, but today his mind was elsewhere.

He stood before a mirror that ran the full length of the inside of the dark pine wardrobe door, his brown suit hanging from the outside whilst he fixed his silver-grey hair with the usual brylcreemed slick back.

George had run things in Stepney since the late fifties, when the twins came to prominence. Now they were inside, and he was worried. Though he didn't like admitting it to himself, they were the main reason he was still in charge all these years later.

He'd started out working for an illegal bookie around the back of a tailor's shop and had been sensible enough to save most of what he earned, eventually branching out into lending money to the more desperate gamblers so they could carry on placing bets and chasing their losses after blowing their wages. He made a good few quid and was careful never to charge ridiculous interest which eventually led to problems with a few of the other local loan sharks.

He wasn't a tough guy, but if nothing else, George was shrewd. He made sure his boss got a reasonable cut of the profit from his repayments so when there was a bit of bother, he always had backup. He was able to stay protected and eventually amassed enough to invest in some of the local pubs and businesses. It was this financial acumen that brought him to the attention of the twins when they emerged from Vallance Road and cast their eyes over the surrounding areas. He'd suggested the partnership to them and although they preferred to call it an arrangement, it'd proved to be mutually beneficial over the years. Their protection and patronage in exchange for a decent cut of the profits. As they took over more and more venues and establishments, they passed the day to day responsibility on to him to the eventual point where he was seen by most as the local guvnor.

As he was putting on his suit, Marjorie came in with his tea and toast. Setting down the tray on the bedside table and walking across the room to fix his tie, the same way she'd done every morning for years. He looked at his wife whilst she fiddled around with the knot, straightening it and making it a little too tight as always. A thin but firm woman with a slightly pinched face and pointed nose, she'd always made the best of herself and kept a very neat appearance, today wearing a pale blue dress with floral imprint and a little make-up but not overdone.

She'd always understood him and his way of life, never complaining even when times had been hard. But that was all a long time ago now, and she'd enjoyed the finer things for many years. She'd made this house a home and looked after him well. He was no oil painting and knew he was lucky to have her, and although he could always have had some young dolly-bird from one of the clubs, they'd only be with him for his money and status. He was far too sensible for that sort of caper.

They'd never been blessed with children, but like everything else in their lives, Marjorie accepted it without complaint or question. Occasionally he felt guilty for not being able to give her what he knew deep down she most desired, but he wasn't going to have some doctor poking around at her or asking him personal questions. It was just the hand they'd been dealt.

Despite this, he was a contented man. But was that all about to change? He was lost in his thoughts as Marjorie smiled at him and said "there you go dear, all ready for the day ahead. Don't forget your tea and toast before you go". If she shared his concern, she wasn't showing it.

The same tea with four sugars, two rounds of toast lightly done, and strawberry jam. Raspberry if she was feeling adventurous. The same thing for years, and he loved that.

She left him alone by the bedside table to eat his breakfast, slowly and methodically. He never rushed anything. It was part of what made him what he was. Safe, steady and secure. After finishing his toast, he got up and took his tea over to the bedroom window, looking out towards Stepney Green. He'd always thought this one of the best views in the district, at least until they'd knocked up those bloody tower blocks. The Green was still picturesque on most days, whether bathed in sunshine or smothered with light mist. It was a clear day today and that cheered his mood a little.

Henry would be round to pick him up in a few minutes time so finished his tea, placed the china cup back on the tray and took it out to the kitchen where Marjorie was clearing up. He leaned in and kissed her lightly on the neck. It was an unusual thing for him to do, and she sensed his worry from it. She turned to look at him and said, "Is something bothering you dear?"

George smiled at his wife. "I'm fine. Just a busy day ahead."

Although nothing further was said between them, they both knew this news about the Kray twins would change things, either temporarily or permanently. She wondered whether she should broach the subject of retirement but thought better of it. Men like her husband didn't often retire. Some managed to get out in one piece, with a bit of money and a little place in Spain or somewhere else hot. But not many. Most ended up looking at the concrete walls of a prison cell, or worse. She shook all these thoughts from her mind and went back to concentrating on making the worktops gleam.

The unspoken remained so. George kissed his wife again, this time on the cheek as he normally did, and left for the day. As she stood in the kitchen and listened to the front door click shut, somewhere deep inside she felt something she hadn't done for many years. Fear. For him, for herself and their future. The only hope she felt was the hope he'd return home to her tonight.

*

Alfred Kemble was an early riser. By the time other people were having their breakfast or leaving for work, he'd already been busy for at least an hour. It meant the job of driving and minding him was dreaded by everyone in the firm. Everyone except Tugs who'd picked him up this morning and taken him to the office. If you could call the nicotine-stained, windowless back-room of a boozer containing a battered desk, two rickety chairs and a rusting metal filing cabinet an office.

Also sat in the office was Teddy Nicholls. Tugs had picked him up from his bedsit just before first light, gently persuaded him to come for a short ride and had him locked in the boot of his car until they'd settled in for the morning.

Tugs stood in the doorway looking down at Nicholls and thought the man was either very brave, bordering on stupid or simply didn't realise the seriousness of the situation. It made him laugh to think how these chancers always seemed to believe they could talk their way out of anything. He looked the man over and wasn't impressed. Nicholls was the wrong side of forty, with a thinning, dull-grey quiffed hairstyle, wearing a faded red and black checked donkey jacket and black jeans stained with Christ knows what. Pale, glassy eyes, broken veins on his cheeks and a blotchy red nose revealed years of heavy drinking. It was an unfortunate part of their business, thought Tugs, that they had to deal with people like this.

Kemble looked at the man sat opposite and smiled. Seeing people in this state brought him a great deal of pleasure as he knew from experience that Nicholls lazy disregard for his current plight would shortly be replaced by something else entirely. He'd been in this situation a million times and the outcome rarely altered.

"Now then Teddy" said Kemble, "it's taken me a few weeks to catch up with you, but you really didn't think I was going to let this go, did you?"

Nicholls briefly made eye contact before lowering his gaze to focus on the desk. "No Mr Kemble. I was going to come and see you, honestly. It's just that things have been a bit…"

Kemble put one hand up to stop him in his tracks. "I don't think you've ever said or done anything that's honest in your entire life. So, let's not play silly buggers shall we? It's going to be a long day and I'd like to get this settled quickly, if you don't mind?"

Teddy Nicholls had several immediate thoughts about how this might be settled and none of them involved him walking away in the best of health. Kemble decided to let him stew for a moment before he spoke again. He looked up at Tugs. "What do you think we should do with Mr Nicholls here? After all, we can't have people thinking I've gone soft."

Tugs smiled slightly and played along with the little scene. "No, we can't have that boss. We can't have people thieving off us and taking us for mugs."

Nicholls looked up at Tugs quickly before turning back. "I got into a bit of bother and needed some quick cash. I didn't think it'd be missed for a few weeks. I was going to pay you back."

“Oh, you’ll pay it back son. With fucking interest”. There was ice in Kemble’s voice now. “I don’t mind giving out loans at the going rate, but I do like to fucking well know when I’m lending. What I cannot have is people in my employ using my money how they like and whenever it suits them. What is it? Don’t I fucking pay you enough?”

“No Mr Kemble, I mean yes, you do” stuttered Nicholls who was quickly losing any remaining confidence that he was going to get out of this one. “It won’t happen again boss, I promise.”

“You’re quite right, it won’t” replied Kemble with enough venom to let Nicholls and Tugs know the moment had come. “You can consider your employment with my organisation officially terminated from this point forward. Tugs will give you your cards.” He looked up at Tugs and nodded. Tugs flicked the switchblade open.

“Please Mr Kemble...” pleaded Nicholls. He put his hands up to protect his face, so Tugs sliced along the top of his thigh, opening a wound that ran almost up to his groin. Nicholls hands instinctively grasped at the wound, trying desperately to keep it together. Blood flowed over his hands and down the chair leg. Tugs saw the opportunity and moving from behind, sliced open the side of Nicholls face.

Nicholls screamed and he forgot all about his thigh. Now he was trying pathetically to stem the blood from the long gash that ran along his cheek, finishing just under his right ear.

Kemble watched impassively as Nicholls slumped to the floor. The blood continued to run from his wounds and started to pool on the floor as he writhed about. Tugs thought about opening a third slice but the floor was already becoming a bloody mess, so he put the boot in a few times, slipping slightly on the last one, then dragged Nicholls the short distance across the corridor and through the back door, leaving him slumped in the alleyway outside. The man would probably be alright to drag himself out onto the main road where some good Samaritan might take pity on him. He wouldn't bleed to death, hopefully.

Tugs came back to the doorway and lit up his first cigarette of the day. He always fancied one after a bit of violence. Smoke began to fill the small space and it there was a metallic smell from the blood smeared over the floor.

Kemble had also lit up whilst he was waiting for Tugs to return. He looked up and blew a bit more smoke out into the foggy air. "Get one of the boys in to clean this mess up, and make sure they don't miss anything by the back doors. And get Fuller down here. I've got an errand for him."

"Yes boss" Tugs replied. But he continued to lean against the door frame and took a couple of drags before dropping his fag and crunching it out under his heel. As he turned to leave, he heard his boss's voice again. "And you can pick that fucking fag end up. My office is in a proper fucking mess thanks to you. It looks like a butcher's back yard in here."

Great, thought Tugs, he's in a right mood today.

Still, he understood why. Things were going to get difficult and he was bound to be on edge. He picked up the fag butt and left to make the call, flicking it away down the narrow passageway that led to the public bar. Fuller wouldn't like being summoned as a messenger boy, but orders were orders.

After Tugs had gone, Alfred sat back on his chair and stubbed out his own fag end in the ashtray, along with the others mounting up. He felt bad for speaking like that. After all, with peeling, cracking paint on the walls, dust and cobwebs everywhere and furniture that the rag and bone man would turn his nose up at, the odd fag butt hardly spoiled the general look of the place. But it wasn't the time to go easy on people, even with Tugs who he could rely on and most importantly, trust.

Things were going to change. For years, Alfred Kemble had controlled the docks along Wapping and Limehouse. It was a lucrative patch to be defended by any means necessary. In the old days that usually meant flick-knives and toe-capped boots. But the twins had been a different story. He could see straight away they weren't going to be put off by a bit of aggravation and could easily wipe him out if they'd felt like it. So, he cut them in for a decent percentage. They generally left him to get on with it, only sticking their noses in if there was any trouble or if they wanted a favour done which could be a pain in the arse, but necessary to keep them onside.

What had stuck in his craw all these years was that ponce on the other side of Commercial Road. How they could let a man like George Patterson continue to run things over there was beyond his comprehension. He hated Patterson with a spite so all-consuming that even some of his own firm thought he was obsessed. George hadn't earned it like he had. Granted, he'd been shrewd getting in with the twins early on, but he was so fawning that Alfred couldn't understand for one moment why they put up with it.

Kemble thought Stepney should have been his years ago. It rankled deep inside that the twins had never let him take over. He could have tightened up the operation and made more money for all of them. To him, the Stepney lot were a bunch of small-time con-men who thought the world ended at Commercial Road. But now it was his time. His chance to get what he'd wanted all these years. Controlling Stepney would mean most of the East End belonged to him. And what would follow from that?

Tugs came back to the doorway. "Fuller's on his way boss."

Like everyone else in the firm, Alfred felt uneasy about Eddie Fuller. It wasn't that he disliked the man. In fact, he could be great fun to be around. But he looked what he was. Evil. If even half of the rumours were true, he wasn't someone you'd like to have around for too long. But the man didn't turn his nose up at much and had proven very useful over the last couple of years. Today he'd be useful for running an errand and giving a poofter a scare.

"When he gets here, give him this letter" said Alfred and handed Tugs a sealed envelope. "Tell him to deliver it to Ray Mason. He knows where he lives. And give it to him personally, not drop it in the letterbox. I want to know he's got it and if Mason shits himself in the process so much the better."

Tugs smiled. "No problem boss, I'll make sure he knows."

"Good. It's a simple job but I don't want any fuck ups today. And if Nicholls is still lying out back drag him somewhere else."

"Yes boss" said Tugs.

Tugs left the room again, but the tension remained, and Alfred Kemble lit up yet another cigarette. Blowing smoke into the already foggy air, he relaxed for a moment, savoring the smell and for once, not thinking or scheming. But it wasn't something he could keep up for any length of time. Thinking and scheming were things he enjoyed, and what he was good at. He liked to keep people guessing about his motives, putting them on the back foot and letting him dictate the way things would play out.

Most people anyway. Early on, he'd tried to scheme his way into Stepney, planting little thoughts into the minds of the twins, or at least that's what he believed. But he didn't reckon on their own abilities. He discovered quickly they could out-think most people in his business and had plans of their own, so a few sharp words of warning meant he didn't pursue that strategy for long. From then on, he kept it straight down the line. He'd heard the stories about what they did to people who tried to cross them, or manipulate them, and he didn't want to become the subject of another one.

Now things were different. He could play his games and scheme all he wanted. No one was around to curtail him and by the time he'd finished with Patterson, the poor old bastard wouldn't know if he was coming or going. And very soon he'd be gone.

*

In his basement flat, Henry White was cooking breakfast. He was alone this morning, for a change. The bacon and eggs sizzled in the pan, and the smell wafted up to his grateful nose. He smiled contentedly to himself as the smell would waft up through to the young couple in the flat above. It was sure to annoy the bloke, who he thought was called Tom but couldn't be certain. They'd barely spoken to each other since he moved in last year, and the dislike was instant and mutual. Still, Henry had the satisfaction of knowing he'd done more than spoken to Tom's bird, Beverly. That thought kept him smiling as he plated up.

Henry was nearly six-foot-tall, broad across the chest and very popular with the opposite sex. He didn't see the point of settling down while he could pull a different bird each weekend and sometimes during the week too. His strawberry blonde hair added to the appeal and though he knew one day he'd probably go bald, he was making hay while the sun shone and gave daily thanks to Michael Caine. Ever since that film 'Alfie' had come out, his popularity with the birds had shot through the roof. Personally, he couldn't really see the resemblance, he was rougher around the edges and thought he looked more like Roger Daltrey, but he wasn't going to question it or complain.

He wolfed down his breakfast, polished off a quick cup of tea and went for a shower, as he didn't want to go out smelling of bacon when he picked up his boss. He was George's driver, bodyguard and one of his top lieutenants. He'd been loyal to the man over the years and carried out his work without question or debate. If it was asked, it was done and as a result he knew he was fully trusted, or as fully as you could ever be in this game.

He wondered what the rest of the chaps were thinking this morning. But most of all what was going through his brother's mind. They'd always been close but could really wind each other up at times. The years after Harold first joined the firm had been the best. They were real brothers in arms back then and the competition had been over who could drink the most or pull the best-looking birds on their endless nights out. They'd fought side by side in pub brawls and even done a few more professional jobs together, teaching one or two tearaways a lesson they wouldn't forget in a hurry.

In recent years there'd been a bit more distance between them. Some of it was down to natural progression; Harold settling down with Paula while Henry continued to enjoy the bachelor's lifestyle. There was also Harold's ambition and growing resentment towards their boss and how the firm was being run. It simmered under the surface and Henry worried it might one day come to a confrontation. Blood was thicker than water, but it would go against everything he stood for to side against his boss. He hoped it wouldn't come to that.

The whole firm knew Harold White was the one on the rise and who'd eventually take over from George. Either that thought Henry, or he'd end up with a bullet in the back of his head. Harold's strength could also be his weakness. He was too headstrong and rushed into things. In some situations that was the way to go but occasionally a little more tact and patience was called for. This was one of those times.

And then there was Ray. Why his brother enjoyed the company of that lairy poof was beyond him. Yes, Ray could be entertaining in his own way, but the public flaunting of his sexuality made Henry uncomfortable. Bringing his boyfriends to the clubs and dressing like a fucking explosion in a Carnaby Street boutique. It wasn't right. If one of the chaps bought a bird to the club and she made a scene, she'd end up with a slap and that would be the last you saw of her, so it shouldn't be any different for Ray, having those young men flouncing around making a show of themselves. He should get them into line, make them behave properly, but he just seemed to enjoy the attention it brought. Even Harold had to tell him to reel it in on occasion.

Henry was unsure about how reliable Ray would be when things started to get difficult. The man looked out for himself first and foremost, and only did what made him happy. Who was to say he wouldn't stitch them up if the offer was right?

Henry chose a light brown suit to make the most of his complexion, topped off with a pale blue shirt and dark blue tie. It didn't occur to him that his vanity was no different to Ray's, just directed in another way.

He walked up the steps to the pavement outside, taking a quick look back at the windows of the flat above, but there were no signs of life. He got into his white Triumph Vitesse and headed off on the five-minute journey to his boss's place. On the way over he thought about the day ahead and what his guvnor would be planning. It would be well thought through, he knew that much, and probably the opposite of what his brother was thinking at the same moment. He could see himself getting involved between them, calming Harold down and saving him from himself again.

The traffic was light, so he didn't have much opportunity to mull things over. He parked up right outside the house and opposite the Green. He could have done with a fag but knew he wouldn't have time. He was right. Within seconds George emerged from his front door and walked swiftly down the steps. Henry got out of the car, went around and opened the passenger door.

"Good Morning Henry" said George, "How was your evening?"

"Morning George. Nice and quiet thanks. Just watched a bit of television" replied Henry. He usually downplayed his social life to his boss but on this occasion, there wasn't any need. He'd not been in the mood for a night out. There was too much going on and he wanted to stay sharp.

"When we get to the office, I want you to call round and gather all the chaps to the club this evening. Use the phone in the bar as I need to make some calls of my own." George continued.

"Yes boss."

Nothing else was said for the rest of the short journey. Henry kept his eyes on the road and his mind on the job in hand. The wheels were in motion.

*

The Britannia was a favourite meeting place for the Stepney firm. A three-storey building on the corner of Cable Street, it needed a lick of paint and new carpets but had an impressive brewery mirror on one wall that made it feel more spacious than it was. Strictly speaking it wasn't open to the public this morning, but to men like Ray Mason it was always open. He'd been waiting for the barman to arrive and unlock. Although he'd never seen Ray before, the barman seemed to know who he was and didn't question letting him in for an early start. Perhaps, thought Ray, he knew me by reputation. After all, there weren't many people around the manor who dressed like he did or took that much pride in their appearance. Slim and olive skinned, with shoulder length dark brown hair and a thin handlebar moustache, Ray was a sharp dresser and liked to keep up with the latest trends. Today he was sporting cream corduroy trousers, a thick brown belt and a deep red open-necked shirt. He sat at a table in the far corner, nursing a whisky and thinking he looked the fucking business.

The door opened, and Harold walked in. He clocked Ray and went straight to the bar, bringing back two whiskies. He sat down uncomfortably on a low stool that had seen better days.

"Who's the new face behind the bar?" he asked.

"Dunno, never seen him before. Want me to check him out?" replied Ray.

"Nah, he doesn't look like part of Kemble's set up. Still, better keep out of earshot, just in case." Harold took a sip of his whisky. "I reckon Alf's gonna make a move soon. We need to be ready".

Ray nodded his agreement. "Yeah. Patsy probably thinks the twins are going to break out tonight and we'll all be back to normal."

They both laughed but it was flat and unable to hide the concern that Alfred would draw first blood. He was bolder and though they hated to admit it, stronger. The weakness at the top of their gang had long been a concern but no one wanted to make things worse with a civil war. The Wapping lot would be all over that and they'd be finished.

"Where is Patsy anyway?" asked Ray

"Probably peeking out from behind the curtains in his bedroom window. Didn't look so happy last night, did he?"

"You could see the worry all over his face. I reckon he'll try for a deal."

Harold scoffed. "He's got no chance. They're coming after us. We should hit them first."

"You heard him last night. 'Don't do anything stupid. Wait for my orders.' All that bollocks. He's shitting himself."

"We'll end up in the fucking morgue with him in charge" said Harold. Ray let the statement hang in the air. He wasn't sure it was the right time for a coup.

At that moment, the saloon bar doors opened, and three young lads bundled in, heading for the bar. Harold turned his head to see what the commotion was.

“Three beers mate” said the tallest, and probably the leader. They were all clad in loose fitting denim and cheap monkey boots and all sported shaven heads. Part of a new intimidating breed of young men.

They certainly intimidated the barman, who looked nervously across towards Harold and Ray. The three lads followed his gaze.

Harold half-turned on his stool and spoke. “Pubs not open yet lads.”

“You two are drinking ain’t ya?” the tall one replied.

“Yeah, we are. But you’re not. So, piss off back to school.”

The tall, shaven-headed leader moved away from the bar, but one of his mates had recognised Harold and quickly muttered something in his ear. There was a moment of contemplation as he weighed up his options. Did he lose face in front of his mates, or take this man on and possibly lose more than that? He decided on another way out and instead pointed towards Harold and Ray. “I’ll see you fuckin poofs later. This ain’t finished.”

With that, Harold stood up. He wasn’t as tall or young as this lad, but there was only going to be one outcome. The atmosphere changed in an instant. Ray knew when someone crossed the line with Harold. And this stupid prick just had.

As Harold quickly strode the short distance across the worn pub carpet towards where he stood, the tough-looking lad suddenly didn't look so tough or feel so intimidating. He started backing away and his mates were already halfway out of the door.

"I'm warning you..." he hesitantly started to say, but that was the last thing he said for some time. A fist into the side of his jaw knocked him backwards onto his arse. His hands went up to his face, and he started to make a low, pitiful moaning noise. Harold resisted the urge to put the boot in, and instead picked him up by the lapels of his jacket and turned him toward the door. His two mates were now halfway up the road. Harold threw the lad out of the doorway and he ended up in a heap on the pavement. After a few minutes he pulled himself up and shuffled away, still clutching at his face. Harold watched him go. It would be a long time before that lad spoke or ate solid food again, he thought, and the last time he'd ever visit the Britannia.

Harold returned to where Ray remained sitting. They didn't need to talk about what just happened. Ray motioned over to the barman for another round. Harold hadn't quite finished his first drink but noticed two empties sitting in front of his mate. Maybe Ray was more worried than he was letting on?

The barman brought the drinks over. "Don't worry about them, they won't be back" said Ray, flashing his sly smile at the lad. There was a pause and the youth quickly retreated, obviously as petrified of Ray as he had been of the gang, but for different reasons. Harold was irritated but ignored it. He wasn't bothered about winding up some poxy barman.

“So, what happens now? We just wait?” he asked again without really expecting an answer. He was agitated, his hand was sore, and that little encounter hadn’t improved his mood.

“We finish these, have another one and then go and pay Kemble a visit” said Ray, lifting the glass to his lips.

Harold looked at him incredulously for a moment before replying. “You are fucking joking Ray?”. But for once there was no humour in Ray’s eyes.

*

By the time they'd finished their drinks and left the pub, Harold convinced Ray that paying Kemble a visit was a bad idea. At least for now. In fact, Ray hadn't put up much resistance and Harold wondered if it had just been front.

They emerged into the early afternoon sunshine and went their separate ways. Harold towards his old family home just off Aston Street. He'd knew he'd get his ear bent but it'd be even worse if he didn't pay a visit today. He'd not been over there for almost a week despite Paula visiting almost daily. He couldn't keep blaming work, so the time had come, and the whiskies had helped.

He strolled down the high street, past housewives going in and out of greengrocers and the Jewish butchers, getting their dinners and other bits in for later. It was a repetitive life and most looked beaten down and older than their years, apart from the odd glamourous sort who still made a bit of an effort. Things had been changing over the past decade and colour was entering their world, on their televisions and in the streets. Clothes and signs were brighter, but in the East End there lingered an air of resignation and almost a resistance to this change. The older generation clung to the dark greys and blacks, the threadbare trousers and jackets and acceptance that life would never change for them. But something had been changing over the past few years, a new feeling of opportunity amongst the young. They could be something other than fodder for the factories. Opportunities were emerging all around them, in the docks where the money was good and even further afield in the boutiques and nightclubs of the West End.

Harold felt a bit left behind. He'd soon be thirty, an age at which most men already had a couple of kids, a job and a rent on a flat or house. Well he had the last two, but he wanted something else, something he couldn't quite articulate or grasp, but he knew it was out there. The opportunities were available for people like him, who wanted to go places and build things. What he wanted to build was an empire, for himself and his firm. And the only thing stopping that was the small fact that he wasn't in charge.

He turned off the high street and strolled down the road like it already belonged to him. He kept thinking about his chat with Ray and it continued to bother him. Ray was usually measured, thoughtful and avoided unnecessary violence, so what was with the rush? Maybe he was just guilty of making a rash decision like anyone else, and no more. It was usually Harold, himself that made the impetuous decisions and people like Ray had to rein him back in, not the other way around. So far today nothing seemed to be going the way it was meant to.

He reached the front door of the terraced house he'd grown up in, hoping Paula had left by now. He really couldn't face the pair of them.

Pulling the key on a string through the letterbox, Harold let himself in. He looked in on the living room and nodded to his father who was sitting in the armchair by the window in his vest and trousers. He turned down his paper for a second, raised his eyebrows in a sort of greeting and promptly returned to the racing section. Harold could see the headline on the outside of the newspaper that had blown everything wide open.

He continued down the hallway into the tiny kitchen that looked out on a bare concrete yard and brick wall. That yard where he'd spent so much time with his brothers, Edward, David and Henry. Edward wasn't about much when Harold was growing up and had gone into the army when Harold was still playing with his toy soldiers. These days he was based in Cyprus, popping back on occasion when leave allowed. Henry, the closest to Harold in age and personality, first got him involved in the gang and looked out for him in the early days. They fought each other like a couple of bulldogs but were still the closest of all the brothers. Their youngest, David, wasn't really like the rest of them. He was the one destined for the nine to five, the nice little housewife and kids. Perhaps he should have fucking well married Paula, though Harold.

"Hello Mum" he smiled.

Gladys White was a small but formidable woman. Like most of the women in the area she was the central figure holding a slightly wayward husband in check whilst bringing up her children virtually single-handedly. The second youngest of them now standing before her in the kitchen doorway, beaming his winning smile.

Gladys turned briefly then went back to staring out of the window into the yard and carried on washing up. "Paula's been and gone" she flatly replied.

He brushed this off and sat down on the solitary stool. "Keeping well?"

"As well as can be expected. She got me some bits for dinner did Paula. I said she could stay but she wanted to get home to do yours. She's a good wife to you my boy."

"She's the very best, Mum". Harold tried to conceal the sarcasm but didn't quite succeed.

Gladys turned her head sharply. "Don't give me any of that. She's good to you. Won't find many like her, so you'd do well to treat her a bit better".

"She doesn't go without, Mum" replied Harold, feeling like he was ten years old again. "I know I'm not home much but it's my job. She knows the score". He decided to change the subject. "How's Aunt Flo?".

Harold knew the opportunity to gossip about her sister would be impossible for his mother to resist, and boring as it was, it'd be preferable to hearing about Saint fucking Paula for the next hour.

He put the kettle on and made tea whilst hearing all about his Aunt Flo's new carpet and how could they afford it, so soon after getting that new sideboard? It had to be on the hire purchase. Apart from going on the rob, it was the only way anyone from around here could afford anything decent.

Two more cups of tea and two hours later she'd warmed to him and they'd enjoyed a good chat. He left her with a hug and went back through to the living room. After a bit of small talk about the runners and riders at Haydock Park which Harold knew next to nothing about, he slipped his Dad a few quid for the bets and said his goodbyes. Harold thought a lot of his Dad. The man was far from perfect but unlike a lot of the blokes around this way, he'd always been there for his family and brought a few quid into the house whenever he could find work at the docks. He hadn't spent a lot of time with Harold over the years, probably because he was bored of the routine, having done the same thing twice before. It certainly went some way to explaining how David turned out. The old man was probably sick to the back teeth by the time he'd come along.

He shut the door and headed up the road. As he was walking away, he turned to look at the old place again. Just a small, plain, terraced house with sandy coloured brickwork and a red door that Edward and Henry now needed to stoop to get through. But it'd always been a neat, clean and warm home for him, and for those he held dearest. Despite their faults and the frequent arguments, he'd fight and die for any one of his family. Harold had done his duty for a week or so, now it was time for business. It was time to see Patterson.

*

By the time they'd finished their drinks and left the pub, Ray had let Harold believe he'd talked him out rushing to take care of Kemble. Making Harold think he was out for blood was risky and he wasn't sure he'd pulled it off, but his mate seemed convinced in the end, and that was a relief. Harold had a ferocious temper and if he thought he was being taken for a mug, there was no telling what he was capable of. Just ask that lad, thought Ray. Though he couldn't answer you if you did.

Ray was still going to Wapping. Not to put a quick fix on Kemble. He knew he'd have little chance of that. The intention was to meet Kemble and hear what he had to say. He'd got the message as he left the flat this morning. Ray wasn't a man who scared easily but Eddie Fuller was a different proposition altogether. For a split second, he thought his time might be up, but the man who stood in front of him looking as if he'd do his own parents for a few quid, only pulled a letter from inside his coat pocket, handed it over then turned and left. He knew Eddie had seen that instance of fear on his face and enjoyed it. Ray stared after him as he walked back to his car, then down at the plain white envelope. He went back up the steps to his flat. When he was inside the hallway, he opened it up. The note didn't say much, just asking him to come to the Prince Regent at lunchtime for a chat about something in his interest, and that he'd be safe.

It was a huge risk, but curiosity always got the better of him, so here he was, getting off the bus and walking towards the pub, looking around for familiar faces and wishing he'd dressed a bit less flash. The door opened on creaking hinges and he stepped inside, instantly regretting the decision to come. It was a bright early afternoon but inside the pub the thick, faded red velvet curtains were closed, and the only illumination came from weak wall lights. Alfred Kemble sat behind a table at the far end, shrouded in cigarette smoke, with three of his firm including Ray's new pal Eddie, who was beckoning him over. Ray wondered if this dingy little pub would be the last place he'd ever visit. What a shit place to die. But he walked across the threadbare carpet and sat down like he was meeting old friends.

"Ray. I'm glad you decided to come. How are you? Keeping well?" drawled Kemble in his affected, posh accent that fooled no-one. The man was Wapping born and bred. He held an open cigarette holder out, offering the contents to his visitor.

Ray took a cigarette and accepted a light from one of the men at the table. He looked across at Kemble and saw a typical old-style gangster, with slicked back dark grey hair, a large nose and broken veins across both cheeks. He was wearing a demob style suit with shoulders so wide and square you could land a plane on them and when he smiled, as he was doing now, he looked like a snake.

"I expect you're wondering why I asked you to come here?"

Ray removed the cigarette and replied. "Not for the pleasure of my company then?"

Kemble shifted slightly in his seat but continued smiling. "I thought we could have a friendly conversation, that's all. Now the twins are away, I'm interested to know George's intentions. I understand you're his right-hand man these days."

Ray knew the man was lying. As if he would ever be the right-hand man. "I couldn't tell you. I haven't spoken to him yet" Ray replied truthfully, but Kemble didn't seem to believe him.

"Really? You've not spoken to him? That does surprise me. In that case perhaps you'd like to know my intentions?"

"Go on."

"I've no need for a war, but I don't want George thinking he's the guvnor around here." The posh accent dropped for a moment.

"You've only told me what you don't want." replied Ray, with more sarcasm than he'd intended. He stole a quick glance around the table, but nobody gave away an outward sign of how this was going to go.

Kemble too showed nothing outwardly, but inside he was seething. Fucking well talk to me like that in front of my own firm, in my own fucking pub. Fucking poof. Lucky I don't slice you into little pieces here and now.

But Kemble just smiled again. Ray wondered if he could spot the forked tongue behind the teeth.

The affected accent was back. "Very well Ray, what I want is for you to run things in Stepney. I know this must seem a bit unexpected, but I'm led to believe you're the one with intelligence in your firm and we both know George and I have never seen eye to eye. I need someone I can work with so if you're willing to accept my offer, I'd clear the way for you to take over without too many problems."

Ray put his cigarette out and leant back in his chair. "Do I get time to think about it?"

"I'm afraid not. I'm sure you can appreciate that time is of the essence."

"I'd be working for you then?" said Ray.

"I wouldn't put it like that. I won't interfere with how you run things and would only take a reasonable cut for my services. If South London or anyone else come sniffing around, we might be glad of the mutual assistance."

"And George gets done?"

Kemble frowned in a slightly mocking way. "I'm afraid so. You're a decent bunch of chaps but George is too weak to lead you against the other firms on his own and the last thing he'd do is reach out to me for help. So eventually you'd come under the thumb of someone from outside the East End, and that's not something any of us want. All you need to do is get your friends in line, I'll take care of the rest."

Ray was about to say something, but Kemble cut back in. "Actually, there is one more thing I'd like from you, if we're to have a deal."

Ray waited in silence, already knowing what Kemble was going to ask of him.

"Harold White" said Kemble. "I know he's a friend of yours, but he'll never go along with this. I'm not asking you to get your hands dirty, just stand aside and let us take care of it. I'm afraid he's out of the picture. I'd like your answer by tomorrow morning".

*

Kemble watched Ray leave, then turned his attention to the three men sat with him at the table. Eddie Fuller, Tugs and a man in thick rimmed glasses who looked like a shifty bank manager and known to everyone as Geordie. These were his top men, but Tugs was the only one he could really trust. Eddie, as they all knew, was a law unto himself and Geordie was a working man, which meant he might just be practical enough to join another firm if the circumstances were right.

Kemble turned first to Tugs.

"What do you think? Is he up to it?"

Tugs thought carefully for a moment, considering his answer. In his opinion Ray would go running to Patterson and would never stand by and watch Harold get done in a million years. "I'm not sure boss. He's too loyal to Harold. It might have been better to go after Jack or one of the others."

Kemble let Tugs stew for a moment before putting him out of his misery. "You're right. He might be tempted but he's too loyal to that mate of his. If it was just a case of ratting George out, then I think we'd turn him".

Eddie Fuller, who was never afraid to speak up, spoke up. "In that case why put it to him?"

Kemble was annoyed at the direct questioning, and more so that they hadn't grasped what was going on by now. "To put the cat amongst the pigeons, as they say. I've no intention of letting Ray Mason run Stepney, or anyone else on their firm for that matter. The only person who's going to run Stepney is me and they'll either fall into line or we'll pension them off."

They were all relieved to hear this. For a moment they thought their boss had gone soft. Kemble continued. "It's my guess he'll go running to his mate, but even if he doesn't, word will still reach George's ears. At best they'll splinter, then we pick up the pieces, and at worst it'll sow some doubts and suspicions. Either way it'll make our job easier if they're looking at each other rather than at us when we come for them."

As he watched them all mulling things over in their own ways, Kemble thought to himself. He couldn't believe Ray had been so stupid as to visit him on his own patch. They could easily have topped him but there wouldn't have been much benefit. He'd been banking on Ray's vanity and curiosity winning out over his suspicion and been proved right once again.

Eddie couldn't be bothered with it all. He was just waiting around until things got moving, then he'd step in and do what he was best at, earning a decent wage putting one or two of the Stepney lot out of the game. He couldn't care less who was in charge so long as someone paid for his unique services.

They finished their drinks and got up to collect their coats. As they were leaving, Kemble took Tugs to one side. "Tomorrow morning, first thing, I want you to make a call and put the boys in blue in the picture about Ray's travels. Ask for Lewis at Limehouse. He picks up an occasional earner from Stepney so he's bound to pass the message on."

Tugs nodded his acceptance. He'd do what his boss asked although for now it was just one phone call after another. But the time would come for the heavy work and when it was all sorted out, they'd have the East End in their pockets.

And for his own part, Alfred Kemble was delighted. His plans were working out perfectly.

*

Harold didn't have to wait long to see George. They'd been ordered to meet in a private upstairs room in one of his clubs later that afternoon. When he arrived, most of the firm were already there and a short while later Ray turned up. Harold could see straight away there was something not quite right. He looked edgy and was unusually quiet.

A large mahogany table and elaborate chairs dominated the room and a few large paintings adorned the walls, with thick gold framing landscapes and vistas, mainly set in foreign lands as George preferred. For the rest of them sat around the table, it wasn't really to their taste. They were more familiar with the view from Southend pier.

George had been skulking around in another room, so he could make an entrance and not be seen to be kept waiting. When he finally entered, he was flanked by Henry who nodded solemnly over to Harold as they sat down. They took their seats and the chatter quickly died away. Patterson leaned forward, rested his elbows on the table and spoke.

"They've given the twins thirty years each."

Not much phased these men, but around the table there was genuine surprise. No one was expecting a stretch like that. Child killers got less. It took a few minutes for the noise to die down again.

"So, what do we do now?" asked Jack, addressing no one in particular.

George Patterson stood up from his chair at the head of the table. He wasn't the tallest or broadest man. In fact, he looked ordinary. In his late fifties, with thinning hair and a ruddy complexion he didn't look like kind of man to be leading a London gang. Now the power base that had underpinned his little empire was gone, and he was as worried about his own firm as he was about Kemble or any of the other firms across the capital.

Ray glanced over at Harold, who's stare remained firmly on his boss, waiting to hear what their next move would be. They'd all judge George Patterson by what came next.

George smiled. "We need to act quickly and decisively. I've spoken to Alf Kemble on the phone this afternoon. He thinks South London are going to make a move and wants us to stand firm with him. We can all keep our share, and nothing changes."

You fucking idiot, thought Harold and probably most of the others around that table. How could their boss be so dense as to take the word of a man who'd wanted him gone for years? Nothing had come from South London since the twins had been arrested, so why start now?

Jack was the first to speak up. "Who's in charge then George? When we go up against South London."

There was an element of sarcasm they all recognized as the first subtle but direct challenge to Patterson's authority. Jack Ford was nobody's fool. He was sharp and could make mischief when it suited him.

All eyes turned back to George. This was the first stab at his leadership. A tester to see how he responded. His answer didn't surprise anyone.

"We keep control of our own firms. I'm still in charge of Stepney."

The disappointment was almost palpable. They all knew you couldn't have two guv'nors. One would always emerge ahead, and it was obvious who that would be. They'd be working for Kemble in no time. Only the man at the top of the table seemed oblivious to that fact or unwilling to entertain it.

Patterson sat back down and there was a bit of cross talk before Harold stood up. He leant forward and looked directly, and down, at his boss.

"We've got to go after Kemble. How do we know South London are planning to hit us? No one's heard a word, and they've been as good as gold for the last few years. He wants East London and I'm not working for that arsehole."

George Patterson tried to sound firm. "You work for me Harold, and you'll do what I tell you. If we go after Kemble now there'll be a war and the other firms will walk all over what's left of us."

If he'd just left it at 'you'll do what I tell you', he'd have regained some respect around the table, but trying to justify himself was a mistake. At times like this, the boss didn't need to justify himself.

Until now, Ray hadn't said a word. He touched Harold's arm, motioning for him to sit down before he addressed his boss diplomatically. "No one's disagreeing with you George. We know it'll get messy if we go to war, but you can understand why we're worried."

"I've got a sit down with Kemble in a couple of days" replied George "Nothing is to happen before then, understood?"

There were a few murmurs, but no one was convinced. Ray carried on. "Alright then George let's see what Kemble has to say and we can decide from there. Why don't we all go and have a drink now? I'm gasping."

Patterson got up and signaled the meeting was over. But in Harold's mind things were very fucking far from over. As they filed downstairs into 'The Pretty Maid', an illegal gambling and after-hours drinking club, Harold brooded over the unsatisfactory ending. He wondered why Ray closed things off so quickly when there was so much to be sorted out. It was one of many things Harold wanted to have out with his old mate, sooner rather than later.

It was the typical sort of club that catered to a typical sort of person. The sort of person who didn't know when they were finished, or didn't want to stop, either after the pubs had closed or they'd blown the last of their wages at the card tables. It was sparse but functional inside, with the occasional effort at extravagance that just looked out of place. In a few hours it would be filled with smoke and subdued chatter, but for now just the members of George's firm hung around the bar while the staff went around setting up tables. George had his usual single gin and motioned over to Henry that it was time to leave, but Henry had persuaded Ginger to do the drive tonight. He needed to speak to his brother.

After his boss had left, Henry made his way over to the bar where Harold was talking to Jack. It soon became apparent to Jack that he was the spare part, so he moved off to find someone a bit more engaging, leaving the brothers to talk.

"What the fuck was all that about Aitch?" said Henry.

"All what?"

"That little performance upstairs. What are you doing questioning George in front of everyone? He's trying to sort this out and you're undermining him."

Harold could hardly believe his ears. He knew Henry was a bit of a company man and for some reason, held a lot of respect for their boss but there were limits. He snorted his derision.

"You call that sorting things out? We're a fucking joke and Kemble knows it".

Henry hissed his response through his teeth. "So, you think you know better? Think you know more than someone who's run this firm for the last fifteen years. I hope you're not thinking about doing anything stupid."

Both men were trying to keep their voices down and were out of earshot from the rest, but those standing nearby could tell something was brewing. They'd learned to recognise the signs.

Harold didn't rise to the bait, so Henry continued. "We do as George says. I'm going to this meet so just leave it to us to sort out. What makes you so certain Kemble wants to take over anyway?"

"Oh, come on 'Enry". Harold was getting exasperated now. "You're burying your head in the sand, same as George. Kemble always wanted this manor and now the twins have gone away we've got to fight for ourselves. Only it seems some of us might not have the bottle."

Henry squared up to his younger brother. He stood a good few inches taller but that didn't make much difference. Over the years, in all their tear ups, neither ever really came out on top. The rest of the firm and some of the staff were starting to look over with interest, wondering who was going to snap first.

But it was Ray, yet again the peacemaker, who came between them. "Pack it in the pair of you. If Wapping are coming at us, they'll have two less to deal with by tomorrow morning."

It just about defused the situation, at least for the time being. It might continue later tonight or another time, but by then it wouldn't be Ray's problem. His main motive was to have a conversation of his own with Harold, and that wouldn't happen if he and Henry were tearing chunks out of each other. It was a conversation he wasn't particularly looking forward to, but this seemed like the best opportunity, before too much booze had been consumed.

He gently led Harold away from the bar. Eric and Don had twigged Ray's game and helped him out, coming over to keep Henry occupied.

As they walked away, Ray turned to Harold. "I need to have a word with you about what happened upstairs".

"Yeah, you do. I am not happy about that Ray."

"None of us are happy about it 'Aitch, but we need to be careful. If Patsy thinks he's going to be toppled, he might do something about it."

"You're joking, aren't you? He's about to get done over by that old cunt down the road and he's sitting there like nothing's changed. It'd be worth winding him up just to see him take some fucking action for once".

They sat down at a small table by the wall. This moment was a risk, but one Ray knew he needed to take. He didn't know how Harold would react, especially with the mood he was already in tonight. Someone started the jukebox and Tony Newley came warbling in the background as Ray leaned forward. Good timing Tony, he thought.

"I've had a message from Kemble as well".

Ray decided not to tell the whole story. Informing Harold that he'd been visiting pubs on another manor might be a step too far.

"He called and told me what we're all thinking, that he's planning to do Patsy. He wants me to take over."

There was silence while Harold absorbed this. Ray waited. Harold looked at Ray, who couldn't take the prolonged silence.

“I managed to wriggle out of giving him an answer for the time being, but it looks like the writings on the wall for Patsy whatever happens. What do you think we should do?”

For the first time in years, there was more than a hint of irritation from Harold towards his best mate. “We? I thought he’d phoned up and asked you?”

“Come on ‘Aitch, I’m putting my bollocks on the block here. Kemble is playing us off against each other and you’re the only one I can trust. I know he doesn’t really want me in charge. We’re both probably on the same list as George.”

Harold seemed placated. “Yeah, sorry Ray. I’m not thinking straight.” He looked around the room, suddenly worried about the walls having ears. “Look, not here okay? Let’s have another scotch and slip away.”

They had another scotch, then Henry came across with Eric in tow and they had a couple more. Both brothers keen to put their earlier conversation behind them, much to everyone’s relief. Eventually, Harold made his excuses and left. Ray followed soon after, but not before he’d had another drink.

As he turned into the side road outside the club Harold was waiting. “Fuck me, you took your time”.

“Got to make it look good ‘Aitch, we don’t want to start any rumours do we? What would Paula think?” Ray smiled, and Harold returned it.

They strolled through the dark Stepney side roads, the street lamps casting weak yellow light on small areas of pavement. They walked slowly and casually in the near darkness, not worrying for a moment about anyone lurking in the shadows. The streets belonged to them.

They walked for a long time, occasionally going down roads they'd already passed, but careful not to venture back towards the club. Although Ray had the most to lose, it was Harold who held sway in the conversation and by the time they reached Ray's place, a plan had been hatched.

Harold walked the short distance round to the modern, low-rise flats. It was getting late now, but he stopped outside for another fag and a think. He looked up at the few lights illuminating the windows of the white and brown building in front of him and felt relieved his flat wasn't one of them. She would be in bed, hopefully fast asleep by now.

He didn't know how he was going to sell this to Henry, never mind about the reaction from the rest of the firm. When push came to shove, would they back George despite knowing change had to come? It was the only way they could take Kemble on. All these thoughts continued going through his mind as he finished his fag, crushed it under his foot and made his way to the entrance. He didn't have the answers but knew one thing for certain. He needed his bed.

Bow, 1956

It's a bit of a dive, but far enough away from prying eyes. The landlord seems glad of the money, even if most of us ain't old enough to buy a drink legally. The weak afternoon sunshine only penetrates the grimy windows enough to show the dust in the air, and the place is virtually empty and silent apart from our little group.

I'm sat with my older brother Henry, and my mates Ray and Jack, celebrating my sixteenth birthday. We're all on our second pint but I've noticed Henry trying to drink a bit quicker than the rest of us. Trying to prove he's the big man. I smile to myself but won't say anything cos I don't want to piss him off. After all, he's paying.

The beer is fizzy and tastes a bit metallic. Henry wants to go up and complain but I stop him as we could get kicked out and we'll have to go home or find another pub that turns a blind eye. And I can't be doing with the hassle. He doesn't protest and goes back to showing off his money and flash new clothes.

We all know where the money's coming from. Even Mum. I heard her going on to Dad about it the other night, but they won't say anything to his face. He's been working for that bloke at the club for a couple of months now and the extra cash is coming in right handy. Mum will moan and worry, but still take a few quid when it's offered, all the same.

So, the beer's a bit crap but so what? It's having the desired effect. I'm feeling brave, so I decide to ask Henry about his new job.

"What do you do at this club then?"

"None of your fucking business." Henry's laughing when he says it, so I reckon he probably wants me to carry on asking.

"Come on. What do you have to do to earn all that wedge?" The other two are interested now.

"When you're old enough you can come in and find out."

Jack cuts in. "I reckon he's a rent boy."

We all crack up at that. Even Henry, which is a bit of a relief. He can be a touchy bastard at times.

"Fuck off Jack." He laughs. "They got you squared up for that job in a couple of years."

"Nah, come on." I persist. "What goes on? I heard a lot of faces go there to plan jobs and that."

"Hark at George Raft over there. Who have you heard that from?"

Now it's my turn to clam up. "Just people. You know." Clever sod has turned the tables on me.

"Anyone I know?"

"Nah, just kids hanging about outside."

Henry laughs at this. "Kids eh? So, what are you lot then?"

Ray holds up his pint and says loudly enough for the landlord to hear "We're over eighteen ain't we?". We all laugh again.

The landlord calls across and we look over, noticing we're the only ones left in the place. "Three o'clock gentlemen. Sup up. I'm closing for the afternoon."

Jack calls back across. "Can I just use your toilet mate?"

"Yeah, go on, but be quick. It's out the back in the yard, next to the gates."

Jack grins at us before finishing his pint and going out the back. After about ten minutes he comes in and we've all finished our beers by now. The landlord is waiting by the door and watches us as we leave but doesn't say anything.

We're out on the street in the bright afternoon sunshine and about to head to the bus stop. But Jack's grinning again and says, "Come on lads, down here." We follow him down a side street and round into a back alleyway that runs behind the pub. Stacked up in front of a large, rickety double gate there's two crates of ale.

"Pick 'em up then" says Jack. "we'll have a little party on the way home".

We're cracking up as we lift the crates between us and walk quickly back down the alleyway towards the street, the bottles clinking together as we go. When we're back at the bus stop, Henry opens a bottle for each of us and we're all standing round, messing about and drinking. Upsetting the other people waiting in the queue.

I'm wondering if the soppy old fart even realises he's been robbed yet.

Thursday 6th March 1969

"Twins: Its Life or 30 Years"

The headlines confirmed yesterday's news reports and a new era dawned over East London.

In Limehouse Police Station, Detective Sergeant Dave Lewis put down his newspaper and sat alone in the far end of the huge main office, filled with desks belonging to all the other Detective Sergeants and Detective Inspectors. It had a high ceiling and huge windows that looked out over the busy dockside streets. The walls were light blue and featureless apart from maps and mugshots, and a large clock above the exit door. Lewis was finishing an uneventful night-shift, yawning, shuffling papers and watching the clock stubbornly refuse to move those last few minutes to eight o clock. He wondered if it had stopped at two minutes before just to piss him off.

Last night had been a rare quiet one. He was a busy man these days. His superior, Detective Inspector Ronald Thompson had been on long-term sick leave for the past few months and it didn't look like he was coming back. That's what three packets of fags every day would do to you. Still, it didn't stop Thompson and wouldn't stop most other people he knew. It was a horrible thought, but DI Thompson's misfortune was his opportunity. He felt bad for thinking it. Ronald Thompson had been his mentor and shown him the ropes during his first years as a detective, even giving him a slice of the pay-offs from local criminals. But times changed, and this was his chance for promotion and big money. He wasn't thinking of the few extra quid in his wage packet. The decent money came from the local firms, and there were bound to be a few vying for his services now.

It had been a long, slow climb up the ladder for him, but finally he was getting somewhere. He remembered back to his days on the beat in the mid-fifties. Things were tough for everyone back then, so he quickly got used to turning a blind eye and taking a favour every so often. He'd been in the right place at the right time, his beat taking him along the docks and the various little benefits they had to offer. And unlike some of those he worked with, he never had any problem taking up those offers when they presented themselves.

When he'd finally made it as a Detective Constable, at the start of the new, swinging decade, he'd yet again been in the right place. Taken under the wing of the then Detective Sergeant Thompson, who was notorious for having all sorts of little deals on the go. If you wanted to be in with the right people and find out the necessary information then you needed to have the right arrangements in place, otherwise there was just too much of a divide and you wouldn't get results. As laughable as it sounded, it was all about trust. That was what the top brass and some of his more straight-laced colleagues failed to grasp.

Now his boss was off in his sick bed and he'd taken over temporary running of the division things had really started to open up. The local criminals were seeking him out, offering this and that and making his life very easy. It'd led to a few decent collars early on which went down well, and he'd quickly taken over where his predecessor left off, letting things run themselves between the local firms and allowing them to keep order in their own little patches. All he asked in return was the occasional result. Just some small-time thief, drug peddler or nonce the local chaps wanted off the streets just as much as the ordinary citizen.

He was startled from his reminiscing by the shrill ring of the phone on his desk. He hoped it wouldn't be something that would mean staying on past his clocking-off time. His eyes were heavy and now the hands had finally passed eight, he just wanted to grab his coat and get home to bed. He toyed with the idea of leaving it, but curiosity got the better of him and he lifted the receiver.

"Lewis..."

"Good Morning."

He didn't recognize the voice. "Can I help you?"

"No Detective Sergeant. But I can help you."

"And you are...?"

"A friend of a friend"

He didn't have time for this nonsense.

"Policemen don't have friends".

"I've some information you might find it useful. A certain member of a gang from Stepney has been hob-nobbing with Alfred Kemble on your patch."

"Hardly News at Ten is it?"

“A certain Ray Mason was seen sharing a table yesterday with Alfred Kemble. Could be of interest to the people who usually socialise with him back in Stepney.”

“And what’s your interest?”

“Just a concerned citizen.”

“Of course. Well thank you for the information. Anything else you’d like to share?”

“That’s all for now.”

The phone line went dead. It was past knocking off time now, but Dave Lewis knew he couldn’t go home just yet. He sighed in frustration. This wasn’t one of his grasses calling in, it was someone looking to stir things up. They’d gone to the trouble of disguising their voice, but it had to be someone on Kemble’s firm, or in their pay. Whoever it was and whatever angle they were working, there would be people willing to pay for the information he’d just received. He picked up the phone again and dialed out.

*

About the same time DS Lewis was making his call, Harold opened his eyes, sighed and rolled onto his back. Propping himself up in bed, he looked down at Paula who pretended to be asleep. He smiled to himself, reached over for his fags and switched on the Radio. The Animals sang about the House of the Rising Sun.

When he'd finished his fag, Harold got up, put on his dressing gown and made his way into the kitchen.

Paula was up and moving about now. He shouted through to see if she wanted a cup of tea and put the kettle on. He was in a much better mood. For a fleeting moment, he thought about what it'd be like to head the firm and run Stepney. He couldn't deny his ambition to himself, even if he'd tried to keep it from showing in front of the others.

Harold and Paula spent a rare, enjoyable morning together. They even went back to bed for a while, which was even rarer.

Later that morning, Paula was in the shower and Harold sat in the armchair in his dressing gown when the buzzer went. He got up and pressed the button, speaking into the intercom.

"Who is it?"

"Get your hairy arse out of bed lad."

Harold smiled and pushed the release button. Last night all forgotten. A few minutes later Henry came through into the living room. Paula popped her head round the door before they'd had a chance to speak and smiled at them both.

"I'm going into town with Barbara. She wants a new dress. You want anything?" she asked her husband.

He walked over and handed her a roll of notes. "Nah, but you treat yourself love. Have a good time". They smiled at each other again before she left. When she'd gone, Harold turned to Henry, who was standing in the middle of the room with a wry grin on his face.

"What's this 'Aitch? Wedded bliss?"

"Leave it out 'Enry, can't a bloke treat his wife now and again?"

Henry moved on to more important matters.

"I had a call this morning about Ray."

"Who from?"

"Lewis. You know, the DS over Limehouse way."

"Is he on our books?"

"Nah, we bung him a few quid now and then. That's all. He's had word Ray was seen going into the Prince Regent yesterday."

"That's one of Kemble's places? I hear they do a nice ploughmans."

Henry frowned. "This is serious Harold. If Ray's crossed over, then we're right in it. We need to sort this out."

"Alright, let me think." Harold sat down, thought, and worried. Not Ray. He'd come to Harold about this last night and they'd worked out a plan. But he hadn't mentioned going to Rayne's manor.

Harold's mind was going in a hundred different directions. He knew Henry didn't really like Ray, and the fact his own brother was so pally with him. He'd even once accused Harold of being a poof. Just the once though.

What if the information was wrong? It could be someone making mischief. Someone from Wapping stirring things up. There was only one way they were going to find out. Henry finally broke the silence.

"So, what do you reckon then? You think he's gone over?"

Harold stood up. "I'm going to get ready then we'll go and see Ray. There's one way we'll find out for certain."

*

Tugs sat in the dingy office on the other side of the desk from his boss. He'd done the rounds this morning, taking the weekly contributions from local businesses. Nothing out of the ordinary. Just another morning's work, if you could call it that. He couldn't remember the last time he'd had any grief or sob stories. They all knew better than that by now.

He counted out the last of the notes on the desk and pushed the pile across to Kemble, who pocketed it. That was another of his boss's odd ways. No using safes or under the floorboards for stashing money. It was always pocketed and carried round with him until it was time to dole out to the chaps or make some other payment. The rest just went home with him.

Kemble looked across at him. “And that other business?”

“Yeah, no problem. Message received and understood.” Tugs replied.

“You think he clocked who you were?”

“Don’t think so. Asked who it was but didn’t guess at any names.”

“Good.”

Kemble sat silently for a short while. Tugs waited for his boss to speak again.

“George should’ve got the message by now.”

“It’ll reach him one way or another boss.”

There was a hint of sarcasm in Rayne’s response. “Well let’s hope it reaches him soon. I want them at each other’s throats before we make our move.”

Tugs wondered what that move would be. His boss had talked of plans, strategies and moves but little detail had been forthcoming. He felt disappointed he wasn’t trusted enough to know a bit more than the rest of the firm but guessed that was how Kemble had always operated and it wasn’t anything personal.

His boss continued. "If we can sow a few seeds and have them looking at each other instead of us we'll be able to move in quicker. This is my chance. Our chance. We can take over the East End and from there who knows?"

"South London?"

"Don't be fucking daft. I'm not venturing into Indian country. They can keep that shithole. I'm talking about the West End. The twins had interests over there and its rich pickings. Just a couple of Maltese to get rid of down in Soho then we can move in on the Casinos. It's all there just waiting for us."

Despite his natural caution, Tugs couldn't help but get swept up with his boss's optimism. "That's where the big money is?"

"Yeah" agreed Kemble "easy money too. All legit. Well, mostly."

"You want me to find out if there's any news from Stepney?" Tugs asked.

"Leave them to stew on it. Patsy's going to be begging for this meet come tonight. And we know what'll happen when he shows his face."

Tugs knew.

*

Paula was desperate to take the wad of notes out of her purse and count it, just to see just how much fun she was going to have in Piccadilly, but she didn't want Barbara nosing or getting jealous. It would be more than enough anyway. They sat on the top deck of the bus, chatting and gossiping, and looking forward to a good wander round the shops. Eventually the conversation came to a natural pause and Paula looked out of the window as the streets passed, becoming busier and more upmarket as they went along. She thought about the morning with Harold and wished it could be like that more often.

She understood the situation. Harold wasn't doing a nine to five job and although there were benefits, there was also the obvious down side. She knew that one day there would be a knock on the door, and it'd be the police, either to say her husband wasn't coming home or to nick him. One day sooner or later, she'd be on her own.

It'd been great for a while, all parties and days out, clothes and jewelry. And their beautiful, modern flat. But as each day passed, she craved the normality of her friends lives more and more. They didn't have the best outfits, the designer labels or endless nights out. But they had peace of mind, something she'd never have. She knew she was trying to turn her husband into something he wasn't and even though she continued trying, causing rows and tension, she accepted it was ultimately pointless. Harold White was born to the life he led and wasn't going to walk away from it to start doing shifts at Fords or open a fruit and veg shop.

She was jolted back to the here and now by Barbara. "Ere' Paula, get your ticket ready. He's coming up the stairs again". It was the third time the conductor had come upstairs to check tickets and on both previous occasions he'd asked to see theirs. They knew why. He couldn't take his eyes off Paula. Barbara made a joke of it after the second visit but inside it rankled, as it always did when they were out, and glamorous, fashionable Paula got all the attention even though Barbara was the more naturally pretty one. The bus was getting busy now, so it took him a while to get to them, but eventually they knew he was standing there beside their seat. They both looked forwards, saying nothing. A few awkward moments passed.

Eventually the man spoke. "Can I see your tickets please ladies?"

Barbara sat nearest so turned and piped up first. "Again? This is harassment this is."

"It's my job madam. I can't remember your destination and you could have gone past your stop by now".

Paula looked over and up at him. She guessed he was late-thirties, maybe ten years ago he'd have been half decent but clearly hadn't taken very good care of himself. The beginnings of a gut stretched at his shirt and pushed his tie to one side, and he needed a shave. She gave him her brightest, winning smile, and said "If you don't fuck off right now you dirty fat bastard, I'm going to punch you right in the bollocks."

She'd picked up a thing or two from living with a husband like hers. It had the desired effect. The ticket collector went bright red and quickly shuffled off to the next row of seats before rushing past them and back downstairs. And that's where he stayed until they got off.

They spent a few hours going around the shops and eventually Barbara found the dress she wanted. Paula bought a new dress for herself but was careful not to get one that outshone her friends. It was nice enough though and would do for Sunday dinner at the in-laws.

They had a spot of lunch together in a café that didn't get many visitors from the East End. It had high ceilings and elaborate wrought iron tables and chairs, all white with the occasional splash of blue here and there, retaining its art-deco roots. They laughed about the bloke on the bus and relived some old memories. Eventually, Barbara left to get home and ready for her evening out. Paula stayed on in the café, happy and contented for now, smoking and watching the other customers while she sipped her coffee as the afternoon faded towards early evening. She thought about Barbara. They'd been the closest of friends since school, sharing good times and bad and even falling out over some bloke in their mid-teens. Both later admitting it'd been the most horrible time of their lives and vowing never to fall out over a boy again.

Unfortunately, that vow didn't hold. They'd spent a couple of years losing touch after Paula announced she was marrying Harold. Everyone knew of his reputation and didn't want her to go through with it, but she was in a whirlwind and wanted to be swept away, seeing only the glamour and romance of that life. Now she knew better and although they'd made up a few years back, they were never quite as close as before. Part of that was the jealousy but if only Barbara knew that feeling was mutual. They could only see the best parts of each other's lives and wanted it for themselves.

Paula paid the bill and stubbed out her fag in the ashtray as she got up to leave. The waiter came over with her coat and held it for her as she slid her arms inside the sleeves. They didn't know who she was but could tell she was someone with a bit of class, from the label in the jacket and the way she carried herself. She disguised her East End roots well.

She still had plenty of money left so got a cab back to Stepney. It would be a lot less hassle than having to deal with dirty ticket collectors and waiting around in the damp afternoon with the crowds heading home. She looked from the cab window as the streets become dirtier and more run down, the closer she got to home. She told herself that one day they were going to get a place in the West End.

*

He lit up again and looked over at the clock. It was almost noon and Ray had spent the morning chain-smoking and worrying. He hated not knowing what was going on and continued to wonder if he'd done the right thing telling Harold about his message from Kemble. Perhaps he should have come clean about going over to their manor but knew it wouldn't have gone down well.

For a second, he wondered if the deal might be genuine and his best option, but even as he considered this, he knew it was ridiculous. Kemble was playing his little games and he was just a pawn. Even if it had been genuine, the rest of the chaps wouldn't accept him as their new guvnor.

Ray had always fancied being in charge and knew he could run the firm a lot better than it was right now. He had total confidence in himself but because of the prejudices of most of the others on the firm he could never lead them. It wasn't about power or respect, but the money would be nice. He'd set himself up in a plush penthouse and do all the entertaining he could handle.

As it was, he had a decent ground floor flat. Tastefully decorated, almost luxurious. Purple and lilac ordained the walls and there were thick carpets throughout. Some people thought it garish or over the top but what did they know? He was unashamed of anything in his life, so bollocks to anyone who thought less of him because of how he liked to live. It was their problem.

It had always amazed him that the one person who didn't judge him was probably the most reactionary and short-tempered of the lot.

He was lucky to have Harold as a mate and knew it'd saved him a lot of hassle over the years. He thought about when they'd first met at school. Back then, he'd been the leader and Harold gravitated to him. Perhaps it was because he didn't really give a shit about anything and was just up for a laugh all the time. Whatever it was, they'd bonded and became firm friends. And he'd never forget the night his best mate went missing during their National Service. He'd been in some crappy, backwater pub in Salisbury expecting his mate to arrive for last orders but that came and went, so he headed back to the base and went to see the NCO who confirmed Harold was missing on an exercise but didn't seem inclined to send anyone to out to search for him.

He'd been furious and stormed out to go and look himself. He'd grabbed an overcoat and torch but hadn't really been prepared and after an hour or so of aimless wandering he was starting to think he might also freeze to death out here when he flashed his torch in the direction of a small group of trees and saw Harold sitting, huddled against the wind and cold. Although it would be stretching it a bit to say he saved his mate's life, it wasn't far off. If he hadn't found him then, who knows whether Harold would have got up again to try to find his way back.

After that, he never expected any favours but Harold was intent on repaying him and would back him up in pretty much any situation, even getting him on to the firm a few years later, despite initial reluctance from their boss and some of the others, including Henry.

It was strange how he could be so close to one brother and so detested by the other. Maybe it was jealousy and the fear he was being replaced as Harold's closest ally that drove Henry White to dislike him so much. It wasn't obvious, outright hatred but it was there alright, just under the surface. Often little more than snide comments or jokes with some of the other chaps, but enough to let him know.

Despite this, he'd turned out to be a real asset to the firm. A good earner with an easy charm and very persuasive when he wanted to be, Ray didn't need to resort to the rough stuff unless it was unavoidable. Violence wasn't his thing, although he was very capable and could be a vicious so-and -so when the mood took him. He preferred to gain someone's confidence and influence their thinking to get what he wanted, and what the firm wanted. He fronted up most of their protection racket, persuading local businesses that an association with George Patterson was to their mutual benefit. He was almost always successful and on the occasion he wasn't, Harold or Jack would continue the negotiation in their own way. The result was always the same.

Sometimes when alone on a job, he'd take a bit extra for himself. Nothing much and not often, just a little sweetener if he fancied some new clobber a decent night out. It was his right, as he was the one sticking his neck out so why shouldn't he take a little bit extra every now and then? It was easy. He'd simply tell one of the places on his collection that the boss needed a bit more this week, for some reason or another he'd make up on the spot. Most of the time they knew they were being spun a line, but no one would ever be stupid enough to grass him up.

Ray was well protected, earned reasonably and had a decent life, but despite all this he often felt unsatisfied. He believed he should be able to do what he wanted, when he wanted, and spend however much he fucking well wanted to. The only problem was he couldn't do it unless he was in charge or well in with someone else who ran the firm.

As he was considering this last thought, there was a heavy, urgent knock at the door. He put out his fag and got up, went across to the bureau and took a small pistol out from the top drawer. Something he kept for special occasions. He checked the clip and flicked off the safety, heading down the short hallway, where the heavy knocking continued. He shouted through "Who is it?"

"It's Harold. Open up, it's urgent".

He knew the voice so flicked the safety back on and opened the door to see Harold but also Henry standing there. Ray's smile faded quickly when he saw the look on their faces.

*

It was mid-afternoon, and George Patterson sat at the desk in his study, away from all distractions. He was busy with his personal finances and for once not dealing with the firm's business. He was almost there. A couple more years, three at most, and he'd have enough to put his plan into action. The plan nobody but he was aware of, to take his beloved Marjorie and disappear off to Spain or Portugal, or maybe even further afield. And leave someone else to deal with all the aggravation.

He'd been laundering money on the side for years. Setting up a nice little arrangement in the square mile with a certain broker who could be persuaded to keep things quiet for a small percentage. And the investments and funds had been building up. He'd soon have enough for a decent villa and a pension that would see them both though their later years in comfort. He was desperate for things to calm down quickly and carry on as they were before the twins went down. Then in few years' time they could have all the gang wars they wanted. It was the last thing he needed now. Punters would stay away from the clubs; some businesses would start to withhold payments and the police would come sniffing around. And that was the best they could hope for. He didn't want to contemplate the worst.

He could understand why some of the firm were agitated and seeking confrontation, but it still annoyed him. And he was especially concerned about Harold. He'd been getting a bit too big for his boots lately and something might have to be done about it. He didn't like resorting to extremes but sometimes it was necessary. And if it came to it, he might also have to get rid of Henry. Blood was thicker than water and that saying often held true. More so than honour among thieves.

He knew most of them thought he was showing weakness, but George wasn't stupid. He knew his best chance was to give in to Kemble's demands and keep most of what he had. He'd lose some income but still have enough to see him through until he was off on a plane with his wife, leaving it all behind them. Kemble would effectively take over, but he'd still have a decent share and eventually be left to carry on running things day to day.

He heard the phone ringing in the hallway. It stopped, replaced by the voice of his wife. She was calling him, holding the phone out to him as he approached. "It's Harold. He wants to speak to you urgently."

George took the receiver from his wife. "Hello? Harold?"

Marjorie went back into the living room but watched discreetly from just inside the doorway as her husband listened. He stood there like that, in silence, just listening and becoming redder in the face. She could see the anger building up in him. His hand turned white as he gripped the receiver ever tighter.

Eventually her husband spoke again. "Bring him to the track tonight. I want him there when I arrive. All the usual arrangements, but I want him in one piece. Tell Henry to pick me up at eight."

Marjorie slipped back further into the living room as the phone went down. The door to the study slammed. So, he'd be going out tonight after all.

Back in his study, George sat slumped in his chair, staring at the wall.

Ray. I should have known not to trust that greedy little shit, thieving off me all these years. I should never have turned a blind eye to it. Well now he's going to pay for every fucking penny he's had off me, and for betraying me to that bastard.

But it was the thought of Kemble that really bothered him. All the talk of deals and arrangements had been lies and deceit. He'd been planning to do him in all the time. Well now things were going to change. Harold and the others would get their war. Once he'd dealt with Ray.

He straightened up in his chair, put his papers away and composed himself. His dreams and plans of flying off into the sun and a happy retirement would have to be put on hold for a while longer. It was time for work.

*

Ray opened his eyes. They hurt. The room was in darkness and he felt the burn of the ropes holding his wrists and ankles tightly to the chair.

He sat there. There wasn't much else he could do. He still had the dull pain in his face from the beating he'd taken earlier. If it wasn't for Harold, Henry might have killed him.

The door opened, and he could make out Harold's unmistakable shape in the frame of the doorway. The shape reached over and switched the light on. It flickered into life with some effort to reveal a grim, dirty back-room filled with rusting greyhound traps, mud covered dog coats and crates of Christ knows what. There was only one window and that had been boarded up. A room with multiple purposes. Ray was tied to a chair at the far end, across from the door where Harold now stood, staring at him. "In here George" he called out behind him.

George Patterson, Henry and some of the firm filed in behind. George stood between Harold and Henry. They all looked at him for a while before George spoke.

"I hear you've been socialising Ray."

It hurt to look up into the stark light, but Ray looked at George, then glanced to Harold and the others. They all just stood looking back at him and the light hurt his swollen eyes, so he lowered his head again. George continued. "You betrayed me. I always thought it might be you. Fortunately, I've got a few loyal men left."

Ray looked up again and this time continued to stare back despite the discomfort.

"Nothing to say for yourself?" George Patterson was becoming annoyed and shouted this time. "You tried to stitch me up! Want my fucking job, do you? You think I didn't know about you skimming off the top all these years? I've let you get away with it and this is how you repay me, by siding with Kemble and planning to have me killed!"

Harold looked sideways at Patterson. If only he'd been this fucking animated last night. He'd hardly ever heard his boss swear before, let alone go off like this. He looked back at Ray, who remained silent.

George Patterson finally ran out of patience with Ray Mason. "Alright Harold. I've had enough. Do him."

Harold took the blade from inside his coat. His face was grim. He knew this had to be done but it was hard to make that final step. He took a deep breath.

At first it felt like being punched. Then tremendous searing pain, worse than the effect of any punch. The knife was long, almost like a bayonet, and it pierced right through to the vital organs. All his breath went, and his eyes opened wide, staring at Harold who looked back at him coldly.

"Why? Why Harold?" That was all he could manage to say through desperate gasps of breath.

"Because you're weak George."

George Patterson was trying to make sense of it all. Still trying to work out why it was happening when Harold pulled the knife out and stuck it in a second time. This time the pain was immediate, and he cried out. He fell to his knees and Henry took hold of his shoulders, purposely looking straight ahead at his brother and not wanting to stare down at the man below him. "One more time Harold" he said without emotion.

Harold put the knife in again. Just below the heart. The result was instant. Henry let go and the body fell limply forward at Harold's feet. He'd knifed people before, given them a real going over and there was always a risk they wouldn't be coming back from it. But this was the first time he'd gone with the intention to kill someone. He looked down at the lifeless body of his old boss lying before him. They all just stood there looking for what seemed like ages.

Eventually, Don picked up some blankets from a shelf and began wrapping them round the body. Harold put the knife inside the blankets, wiping most of the blood from his hands as he did so. They would go together, and neither would ever be found.

Henry was looking at Harold. "You've got blood on your coat. That'll have to go too."

Fuck it, thought Harold, that was a decent coat. Cost me a few quid. He took it off all the same, folded it over and went to put it inside the blankets but hesitated. If things went wrong and they discovered the body, they'd have him bang to rights.

"What's up Aitch?" said Don, still wrapping the blankets round the body.

"I'll take the coat and burn it" replied Harold. He looked at his brother and answered the question before it was asked. "Don't worry, I won't forget".

Harold put the coat down and walked across to Ray, who looked up at him and smiled. "Thank fuck that's over. For a minute there..." His words trailed off.

Harold tried to smile back at him but couldn't. He took out a flick knife and started to cut the ropes.

"You alright Harold?"

"Yeah."

Ray rubbed his wrists. He ached all over now. And even though he was the one who'd gone through all that pain, he was still asking his mate if he was alright. The stress of the situation had made him tired and the earlier beating had started to really take effect. Harold finished freeing his ankles and he tried to stand up, but his legs were dead, and he held on to the chair.

They looked at each other again. "It had to be done Harold".

"I know."

Ray remained on the chair and rubbed his legs to get some of the feeling back into them. Harold walked back across to the rest of the gang who were standing around Patsy's body, all wrapped and bound up. They just stood there, looking down at the body and then at him. Eventually he realised they were waiting for him to give the orders.

He duly obliged. "Don, take the body over to the yard in Dagenham. If anyone wants to pay their respects, they can visit the Tower Block when it's up". Grim laughter followed but Harold wasn't joining in.

"Eric, you clean up in here. Burn the chair and ropes. All of you meet me tomorrow in the Britannia. Eleven o' clock. Don't be late."

Henry and Ray both wanted to say something to Harold, but the look on his face told them otherwise. They all watched him as he walked out, across the track and into the car park. They heard the gravel crunching as his car pull away.

No one said anything, they just got on with their jobs.

*

Henry had gone with Don to Dagenham to help him with the body. They'd left it in the bottom of one of the huge mixers and phoned the foreman from the office. He was to get in early and start mixing up for the foundations before anyone else arrived. If things went as planned, he'd be having a very nice holiday with his family this summer.

They'd used this man before and he'd always been reliable, so they didn't feel worried. Don suggested a drink when they got back to Stepney and Henry quickly agreed. He needed one.

They'd had a few pints, but Don was a family man so was off at closing time. Henry didn't feel much like going home so took a cab over to an after-hours club in the Roman Road. It was quiet and that suited him. He recognised the faces, mostly armed robbers too interested in discussing potential jobs than making small talk with him.

He made a point of chatting to the barman for a little while, in case he needed an alibi. Although not the most reliable witness, the barman would of course insist Henry had been in all evening. Eventually he went and sat in a booth at the back of the club, nursing his pint.

Today's events had left him reeling, both physically and mentally. The first thing that struck him was how knackered he'd got administering that beating to Ray. Although it had been measured and contained, he'd started to get carried away and Harold had to step in before it went too far. He'd enjoyed giving that poof a pasting. Something he'd wanted to do for years. But for the first time it occurred that he might just be getting a bit old for all this.

It had taken Ray a long time to convince him. Harold quickly accepted Ray's version of events, but Henry thought that was more out of loyalty and a refusal to accept his best mate had turned traitor. At one point, he wanted to truss Ray up and drive him straight round to George's, but Harold pointed out their boss wouldn't welcome problems being literally dumped on his doorstep.

Eventually Harold and Ray had worn him down and got him to accept that not only was Kemble playing them all off against each other, but that George's plans would never work. Deep down he already knew it, but it took a long time to admit all the same.

Now he just felt sick. All those years of loyalty and the respect he'd shown George Patterson, gone in one evening. He didn't even like calling him Patsy as he felt it undermined the man, and now he'd held him as his own brother stabbed him to death.

But no one was closer to him than his brother. They'd argued last night and still didn't quite see eye to eye on the whole thing, but Henry had to agree with Harold, and this had been the only way. He wished it hadn't been so and, on the journey over to the dog track he'd tried to persuade them to pension George off. But it was a foolish notion. George had too much pride and would never go that easily. That was the consensus in the car so drastic measures were called for.

On that journey, no one had talked about who would take over once it was done. But Henry knew, as they all did, there was only one candidate. He wondered if this had been Harold's main motive but thought better than to voice that opinion.

Now he sat alone in this sparse little back street hall, drinking steadily but not getting drunk. There was still too much adrenaline for the alcohol to take any real effect. Eventually he'd had enough of sitting there brooding alone. Most of the other patrons had left apart from a couple of hardened drinkers who would probably roll out with the sunrise. He shifted and went to the bar, returning his last empty pint glass. He nodded his goodbye to the barman and left a decent tip on the counter for good measure.

It must have started raining while he was inside and was still drizzling. Henry pulled the collar up on his coat and started to walk along the Roman Road towards Stepney. He passed under the streetlights, hoping to catch a cab but there was hardly any traffic about. He lit up a fag as he walked along, cursing all taxi drivers.

It started raining heavily again just as he turned into his street, so he jogged along and down the steps to his flat. The walk had rid him of any lingering effects from the booze and he was just tired now. As he turned the key, he heard a noise from above. He turned and saw Beverly looking through the open window, the net curtains blowing in the breeze and almost wrapping themselves round her head like a veil.

"Sorry if I woke you up" he called up as quietly as he could manage. He couldn't tell what she was wearing but hoped it wasn't much.

She fought against the net curtains, pulling them away from her face and smoothing out her long brown hair. "You didn't." she replied. “I never sleep well when Tom’s on nights. Just heard a noise and wondered what it was.”

Henry thought she sounded slightly pissed.

“Tom working nights, is he?”

“Started last week at that car factory in Dagenham. He’s a security guard.” There was a little pride in her voice. Her man had a steady job.

He’s not the only one who’s been to Dagenham tonight, thought Henry. He smiled up at her. “Well I’d better let you get back to your bed. Don’t want you sleeping in and missing breakfast with your man, do we?”

She bristled a bit, and he knew he’d got her. She was trying to play a game here, but it was all too easy for him. He’d seen this little routine a hundred times and knew where it almost always ended up. She kept looking at him, so he opened the door. He wasn’t really in the mood. If she wanted it, then just come down and stop pissing about.

“See you then” he said as he made his way in. She didn’t reply, just poked her head back in and shut the window.

He slumped down on his sofa and could feel his eyes getting heavy. But he was keeping himself awake for a few minutes, just in case. As he’d half expected, there was a gentle knock at the door. Henry pulled himself up off the sofa. He’d have to keep himself going for a little while longer.

*

Harold pulled up outside the flats. He turned off the ignition and sat in silence and darkness for some time. He thought. And thought. And smoked.

He remembered the fight outside the youth club years ago, where he'd put that other lad in hospital. He could remember every detail about that night except the fight itself. It'd been an argument between them that developed into a challenge and invitation to settle it on the pavement outside. After making a decent fight of it the lad finally put his hands up as if to say he'd had enough, but it was just a trick and as soon as Harold dropped his guard, the lad steamed in again with his head, smashing it into the bridge of Harold's nose.

After the initial shock, sniffing up and trying to wipe the stream of blood that had started flowing down his face, Harold lost it completely and beat the lad unconscious, but put the boot in a few too many times before he was dragged off. They were all worried at first but luckily there was no permanent damage. Of course, no one, including the lad said anything to the police or gave up any names, but even though he'd gotten away with it, Harold realised he would not have stopped, and in his temper, he was capable of anything, even killing someone.

This time had been different. He'd had the opportunity to come up with the idea, plan it and think about it before carrying it out. He'd almost talked himself out of it a couple of times but knew it had to be done. It was the only way and he couldn't rely on any of the others to keep a steady hand when the moment came. It also meant there would only be one natural successor. He hated himself for thinking about it, but he knew no one would challenge him taking over the firm if he was capable of killing his own boss in cold blood.

He looked at the reflection of his eyes in the rear-view mirror to see if he could notice any change in himself. It was a strange thing to do but he wasn't thinking straight and urged himself to get a grip. He'd have to go up to the flat eventually and face Paula. He didn't know how he was going to react. Was he going to carry on as if nothing happened, cry or belt her one the moment she said anything out of order?

There was only one way he was going to find out. He put out the cigarette in the ashtray, the ash spilling out over the side into the footwell and the edge of his seat. He brushed it away from his trousers and opened the car door, spilling the rest of the ash on the concrete. Closing the door again he looked over for his fag packet to see if he'd any left and noticed the folded-up coat on the passenger seat. Bollocks. He'd meant to stop off at the club and put it on the fire in the upstairs room, but completely forgot and now here he was, staring at it and wondering what to do. Should he drive back over there or take a chance?

He'd have until the morning before Marjorie rang the police to report her husband missing, so he decided to stash it away for the time being, putting it in the boot of his car. He thought better of hiding it in the communal bins or somewhere else nearby in case some early bird neighbour came out with their rubbish first thing in the morning and found it. That would have just been his luck.

Eventually he made it up to the door of his flat. The light from the living room was still on and the television still going.

Paula heard the door and came rushing into the hallway, all smiles. But it soon faded when she saw the look on his face and dried blood on his cuffs. They stared at each other from opposite ends, both knowing that whatever they'd fleetingly had this morning had gone again.

He went straight into the bathroom, leaving her standing there. Although it was obvious something terrible had happened, she knew better than to ask so just turned around and went back into the living room, staring at the television screen but not taking anything in. The flicker of hope had been blown out just as quickly as it'd been lit.

Harold stared at his reflection in the mirror. He looked and felt exhausted. He remembered the mirror in the tiny bathroom of the home he grew up in. The nights it reflected cuts and bruises from pub brawls, straighteners and innumerable other fights. He'd beaten men, put the boot in and smashed bottles over heads. This time it had been premeditated, cold and calculated.

He managed to get the rest of the blood off his hands and from under his nails. It'd dried so took some shifting. He splashed water on his face and looked back up into the mirror, but nothing changed or washed away.

*

Sitting alone on the couch in the well-furnished living room of their well-furnished house, Marjorie Patterson only heard the ticking of the clock on the wall. She'd been on the sofa since dinner time, when her husband had returned briefly to tell her he had some important business to attend to. She understood. It was part of who he was and the responsibilities he had, and things were going to be difficult for a while, she knew that.

She'd sat there, watching television for a while and making herself the occasional cup of tea. Then later listened to the radio, expecting him back or at least a phone call to say it was going to be a late one. As the time passed, thoughts gathered in her mind that she suppressed. It was strange. In all the years they'd been together she'd never felt like this before, worried for him and afraid for herself. The radio continued to play in the background as the thoughts became harder to push out. It began to annoy her, so she got up and turned it off. She sat in silence as the night drew in, not moving to turn on any lights or make any more cups of tea.

Now she sat in near darkness and silence, glancing up at that clock which she could just make out from the moonlight coming through the gap in the curtains. It told her the time was quarter to two in the morning. In all these years, her husband had never been out this late without phoning or somehow getting a message to her. She couldn't hold back the thoughts any longer.

Marjorie Patterson put her face in her hands and quietly began to cry.

Stepney, 1960

I'm shitting myself here. Just waiting.

Henry's upstairs with his boss. They've been up there for fucking ages. At least it feels like that. I'm waiting in the bar, desperate for a drink but I don't want to give a bad impression. The barman and the few punters are all looking at me like I'm a piece of shit. If only this was another time.

Eventually, Henry comes down the stairs and I look across at him a bit too eagerly. I can't help myself. He beckons me across, so I get up and follow him back upstairs. About halfway up, he stops and turns halfway to look at me.

"Don't give it the fucking big one in there okay? He won't be impressed, and you'll make me look a prick for putting your name up."

"Don't worry" I reply, "I'll behave me'self". I try to smile but I'm too nervous.

Henry doesn't say anything else, just turns and starts walking up the stairs to the door at the top. I'm right behind. He knocks and enters. I follow him in.

The geezer is over the other side of the room, standing behind his desk, looking out of the big window over the street. He's obviously trying to make an impression. Doesn't look much though, just some bloke in his forties with thinning hair and a suit that's well made but out of style. After a few seconds he turns around and sits at his desk, motioning for us to sit on the sofa against the wall. It's fucking stupid as we have to sit sideways on to talk to him.

"So, you're Harold. Henry's brother?" he enquires

"Yes, Sir". I reply as I've been told, respectful and to the point.

"Henry tells me you're interested in doing a bit of work for me"

"I am, Sir". Fucking hell, I'm starting to get annoyed with myself. I sound like a right ponce.

"Has he told you what sort of business I run?"

This is where I need to be careful. I can feel Henry watching me.

"A little. Just the basics."

"And you don't mind getting your hands dirty? It can be a bit dangerous at times."

"I don't have any problem with that."

He smiles, and I can feel the atmosphere lighten. I'm sure I can hear Henry exhaling.

"So I'm told. I heard about your little ruction at the billiards hall. That's where you hang around isn't it?"

"Yeah." I pause. I can feel Henry's gaze boring into the side of my head again. "Yes, it is."

"And you're mates with Jack?"

I nod.

"Good. I like Jack. He can be a bit flash but he's doing well for me so far and speaks highly of you."

"He's a good mate. I've got another mate..." I'm stopped by a sharp dig in the ribs.

Patterson ignores this. "Well, let's start you off running a few errands and see how you get on. Henry will let you know when I've got something I need you to do. Just make sure you stay out of any more bother and don't get your collar felt."

I start to reply but he looks down at whatever he's got on the desk and puts a hand up dismissively. It's time to fuck off. As we're leaving, he calls across the room.

"Oh, and one more thing. Try not to smash the billiards hall up again, it's under my protection".

"No, Sir" I reply, again. Three fucking bags full Mr Patterson. I'm smiling to myself as I walk down the stairs. Under his protection? I've been collecting from Sammy's place for about two years without so much as a 'do you mind?'. This geezer's a fucking joke.

As we reach the bottom of the stairs, Henry points to the bar. We go over and get a couple of pints in, clinking the glasses as we toast the newest family member to achieve gainful employment. Of sorts. Henry's pleased for me, but I can tell he's worried too. I can understand as it's his reputation on the line if I fuck things up, but from what I've just witnessed I don't think that's going to happen. The geezer doesn't even know one of his places was being collected from by some snotty teenager for the past two years. I'm smiling again at this thought when Henry pipes up.

"Feeling happy with yourself?"

"Oh, er, yeah" I reply. "cheers for putting a word in for me"

"Don't let me down Harold."

I don't bother to reply. Just take another sip of my beer.

He continues. "What was all that about up there? My other mate?"

"I was putting a word in for Ray"

Henry looks aghast. "Ray? For fuck's sake Harold. First off, it's a bit early to start making recommendations and second, there is no fucking way Ray is joining this firm."

I decide to push it. "Why not?"

Henry affects a soppy, camp voice "He won't want to get his dainty little hands dirty, will he? Might chip his nail varnish." I'm really hoping none of the regulars can hear this, but I shouldn't be. None of them would give Henry any lip.

I know it's bollocks but don't want to ruin things and have a row with my brother five minutes after being taken on. I'll get Ray on the team later. So, I just laugh. "Yeah, alright." And carry on drinking.

Friday 7th March 1969

As he looked out of his window towards the grey Stepney streets, Ray thought about previous night's events. After leaving the dog track, he'd gone straight to the pub, not just to be seen in public by lots of people but to get blind drunk. He'd tried pulling to take his mind off things, but his heart wasn't really in it and he ended up going home alone for a change. The cuts and bruises around his face probably didn't help his chances much either.

Jack and Eric had come into the pub just before closing time, but they only exchanged a few pleasantries before heading off to the back of the bar for a private chat. They weren't keen on his preferences and keeping him on the fringes was one way of letting him know, but he didn't care. Things were settled for their firm and they knew who the new boss was. His best mate. The rest of them could just piss off if they didn't like him or what he got up to. He knew none of them would have the bollocks to say anything to his face, especially now.

This morning he stood at his bedroom window, feeling like shit and wondering what would come next. Would there be any challengers for Harold to deal with? He doubted it. None of the others were as strong as Harold or had the same inner force. No one else in the gang could have done what he did last night.

He got dressed and went downstairs. Plain grey shirt and black trousers today, nothing flamboyant. With the mood everyone would be in, it wouldn't be a good idea to look like he didn't have a care in the world, because he did. He cared about the reaction from Limehouse and if the police were going to come knocking.

Even though they were on good terms with most of the boys at the local nick, they'd be under pressure to ask questions and get some results, and he'd be one of the first they'd come for. He thought Marjorie might have called them this morning to report her husband missing, and they'd guess he'd probably been topped, so there wouldn't be any point in rushing around.

He checked his watch. Quarter past nine. Plenty of time for breakfast before the meet. It would help soak up last night's booze. He wandered into the small kitchen at the side of the lounge and rooted around the cupboards and fridge before settling on coffee and fried eggs on toast. Firing up the grill and putting the kettle on, he thought a little more about the situation and it calmed him. Despite the chaos and suspicion, he was in a good situation. He backed his mate to come through if there was war with Kemble or any of the others. Harold had always been strong and willing to do what was necessary to win. Sometimes he lost his rag and went a bit too far, but no one was perfect. He put the frying pan on the stove and cracked two eggs into it, listening to them sizzle.

When it was all ready, he took his breakfast through to the lounge and settled down on the sofa. His body ached all over now the alcohol had worn off. He dared to think the worst was over and maybe now Kemble would back off, knowing he'd have a real fight on his hands if he took Harold on. He bit into the toast, savoring the thick, runny butter and eggs. It hurt where he'd cut the inside of his mouth during the beating last night, but it was worth it. It would all be worth it in the end.

*

About the same time Ray was tucking into his eggs on toast, Harold was on his fourth cigarette and second phone call.

As soon as he put the receiver down on the cradle it rang. He let it ring a couple of times before answering. It wouldn't do to appear he was rushing to the phone, no matter who was on the other end of the line. The call was from DS Lewis and it was short and to the point. They needed to have a chat and quickly. He knew this would just be to confirm he was now the man in charge and the one who'd be paying their bonuses in future.

He had a busy day ahead and hadn't slept well but didn't feel as bad as he thought he would this morning. The sick sensation of guilt had receded a little, and now he was focused on getting a grip on things, consolidating the events of the night before. Kemble was the one on his mind, and he was sure he'd be in Alfred Kemble's thoughts once he'd got news of what had happened last night, and word would reach his ears quickly.

Paula was pottering about, doing some housework and generally trying to stay out of his way. She knew something had affected her husband deeply since yesterday, and things had changed for them both. Eventually she got the courage to put her hand on his shoulder and was genuinely surprised when he reached up to hold it. He didn't look up at her, and they just stayed that way for a few seconds before she moved her hand gently away and carried on cleaning the surfaces of their pale blue and white worktops.

The feeling of guilt arose in Harold again, but this time for his wife. He worried about the effect this would have on her and whether she was really cut out for this life. In some ways she was perfect for it, being a tough character herself, but he knew that deep down she wanted a life like her friends, albeit with a bit more money floating around if possible. And how could he blame her, after all her friends didn't have murderers for husbands. As far as he knew anyway.

Naturally, his thoughts drifted back again to Alfred Kemble, wondering if he'd still want to take over. If he did, he'd have a fucking war on his hands and would find the new guvnor of Stepney a very different proposition to his predecessor. If it came to war, then so be it. He'd never shied away from confrontation in his life and wasn't going to start now.

But right at this moment, he didn't know what was going to be harder, dealing with Alfred Kemble or his own wife.

*

Later that morning Harold sat at the end of the long table upstairs in the Britannia, holding his first meeting as head of the Stepney firm. It was standing room only. Everyone wanted to be there, to show their loyalty and see how the new guvnor was going to shape up.

He felt better having a sense of purpose and relishing the sense of expectation. This was where he belonged. He stood up and the talk quickly died down. When there was silence Harold looked around the room, at the faces of the men he'd worked with for years. He put his hands flat on the table, leaned forward and spoke with purpose.

"Things have changed. I know you lot want to get back earning as quickly as possible, but nobody here will be earning if Kemble takes over, or at least not earning anywhere as well as you have been." His voice began to rise and get stronger. "I demand loyalty and respect. If you're in this room, then you're here because I want you to be. You've got to be willing to see this through to the end and make whatever sacrifices I tell you to, until it's over and Kemble is out of the way."

He knew he had to get them all onside, but he wasn't about to go down the same route as his old boss, talking about deals and things staying as they had been.

"I'm prepared to talk to him, but only to find out where he wants to be buried. I'm ready to fight, and you need to be ready as well. We're not the pushovers that Kemble or any of the others think we are." He was becoming ever firmer in his words and body language as he went on, leaning a little further forward. He noticed some of the chaps leaning back further or uncrossing their arms. A good sign. He had their full attention.

"I'm not going to concede one inch of our territory. We earned it and we own it. Stepney belongs to us and it always will."

There were clear noises of agreement around the table. Harold went on.

“Jack and Ray are going to call round to everyone later and let you know the plan. You’ll need to get tooled up so see Don on the way out and make sure you don’t get a pull on the way home.”

Some of the men around the table started to shift, but Harold stood up straight and there was silence again.

“I only want people on this firm I can rely on one hundred percent. We’re going to sharpen up this operation, starting with the places under our control. The twins are gone, and certain people on the manor think we’re in trouble so they’re going to start taking liberties. Well no one takes fucking liberties with me. We’re going to make sure they know who’s in charge. All right, get going.”

As everyone started to leave, Harold pulled Don aside to ask about the clear up last night and was pleased to hear everything had gone well. He mentioned the coat in the boot of his car and knew he could rely on Don to take care of that without any fuss.

Harold went down to the bar and a few of the chaps were still there. He was pleased to see Ray and Jack waiting for him. The conversation quickly turned to Alfred Kemble. Harold had spent most of the night thinking about him, and a plan was already forming in his mind. He went over the outline of it with them, careful not to go into too much detail. The lads only needed to know their own jobs.

Eric came back in as they were talking but stood at the end of the bar, waiting for them to finish. He knew better than to get involved in what was clearly a serious discussion. He watched as Jack was politely informed he should get going, leaving Ray and his new Guvnor in a close, whispered huddle. He knew it must be about what was going to happen with Kemble and part of him felt a bit put out that Ray had quickly become the right-hand man in the organisation, but he soon accepted it was inevitable. Ray and Harold had always been close, so it stood to reason. If he could get back to earning, he'd keep his head down and his mouth shut.

Eventually, the discussion was over. Ray finished his drink and left the pub, nodding across to Eric as he went past. Eric reluctantly returned the gesture and walked over to Harold.

"Ready Aitch?"

Harold looked at the dregs of his pint and placed the glass down on the counter. Before replying he motioned across to the barman, who stopped cleaning glasses and came to the other side of the bar.

"Yes, Mr White?"

"Next time I come in, I want to taste the beer. Get the pumps cleaned out."

"Of course, Mr White" replied the barman, a little more enthusiastically this time.

Harold shrugged on his coat and turned to Eric. "I'm ready now."

It's the little things that matter, Harold thought to himself as they went through the doors to the bright sunlight of the street outside.

Eric was driving the blue Cortina with Harold sitting in the back, deep in thought as they made their way back to Harold's flat. The meeting had gone well. They'd accepted him without question or the need to comment and he was starting to demonstrate his authority in small ways without the need to put on a big show. That would only make him look uncertain and desperate. He knew, above all, he couldn't show the slightest sign of weakness in front of his own men right now. Not if they were going to back him in what was coming next.

He was conscious they'd driven in virtual silence since they left the pub. Clearly Eric was wary, and Harold couldn't blame him. He'd seen the look and brief exchange between Ray and Eric in the bar earlier. It paid to notice these things.

"What's the problem with Ray and the rest of the chaps?"

"Problem Aitch?"

"Come off it Eric, you know what I mean."

"It's not Ray himself, it's just his... you know."

"His what?" Answered Harold, knowing perfectly well what.

"You know. Him being a poofter and that."

Harold stayed silent, letting Eric stew. Eventually he spoke again.

"If he wasn't one, you'd treat him better?"

"Come on Aitch. It's nothing personal, just some of the chaps don't like it, that's all."

Harold's tone was cold. "Ray sat there last night bound up to that chair, not knowing if he's going to get done. He stayed firm and didn't shit himself. He's one of us and don't ever forget it."

Eric was immediately apologetic. "Oh yeah, I know. I didn't mean it like that. We all think he's solid."

They both though it best to leave it at that and carried on the rest of the drive in silence. Eric occasionally glancing a worried look in the rear-view mirror.

A short while later they pulled into the car park. Eric turned the engine off and looked around at his new boss. "What time do you want picking up later Aitch?"

"I don't know yet. I'll give you a bell. Make sure you look after the motor, there's a good lad." Harold was smiling as he said this, and leant forward, patting Eric on the shoulder, feeling a little guilty for having a go at him earlier. He needed everyone behind him right now, but it didn't hurt to keep them on their toes.

*

Steam clouded the windows of the Victory Café which sat at the end of a row of bombed out shops and houses. Rusting corrugated iron made up most of the frontage along the road. The premises hadn't escaped the Luftwaffe entirely, and there was a fair bit of damage to the brickwork on the outside, but the owners had made the best of it since the war and looked forward to the compensation they'd get when the council finally got around to demolishing the street.

Inside it was a busy, noisy mixture of young mothers, pensioners and the odd youth who should have been in school. Alfred Kemble sat at a table by the back wall, facing the doorway. He was with Molly, having a late breakfast as they usually did on a Friday. Today they were joined by Tugs, perched awkwardly on a chair, sideways on at the end of their table.

Molly wasn't happy with the new arrangement and her look let it be known. Tugs just sat quietly, wondering if it was just the intrusion, or her being seen with one of her husband's firm in tow, and a black one at that. He let the thought drop, sipping hot, sweet tea and staring intently towards the front of the café. It annoyed him that he couldn't see outside very well, thanks to the steamed-up windows.

He also noticed his boss was even more miserable than usual. George Patterson was dead and there were lots of rumours going around. Most were nonsense, but nobody was sure who'd taken over. Harold White was the popular opinion, but there were some whispers about Ray, and even Harold's brother Henry.

Alfred was thinking along the same lines. Harold would the worst possible outcome for him. He knew he'd have to fight for every inch of ground that should by rights be his and knew the Stepney firm would rally around someone like Harold White. Alfred thought about the angles and possible ways to undermine and defeat him. The man was headstrong and could be forced into a rash move. He pondered on this for a while as his breakfast got cold and the atmosphere around the table even colder. Eventually he realized they'd all been sitting in silence for the last fifteen minutes. He looked up at Tugs.

"All quiet boss" said Tugs.

He nodded and turned to Molly. "How's your sandwich love?"

"It's alright" she said, making it sound like she was only eating this crap for his benefit. "Bacon's a bit underdone as usual."

"You want me to have a word with Mick? Get you another?"

"No. don't trouble yourself. It'll have to do."

Alfred felt bad. Molly was a good woman who never questioned him about his work. Well, hardly ever. Being this picky and difficult wasn't like her at all. He decided to confront it head on.

"It won't be like this for long love. Things are a bit tricky, what with the twins going away and people are out for what they can get. I just have to be careful."

She softened a little, but he could tell she wasn't satisfied with his explanation. Naturally, she worried about him and their future together. And she was nobody's fool. She knew he didn't have a clue how long this was going to go on for, and whatever explanation he provided her with, the reality was bound to be worse.

Mick broke the tension by placing a fresh pot of tea on the table and clearing the plates away, as he'd done every Friday for the past eleven years. He'd heard their conversation from behind the counter just a few feet away, but both plates were almost clear, so the bacon couldn't have been that bad.

After Mick had gone, Alfred talked over their plans for the weekend. He wanted her to go to her sisters in Kent for a few days, just to get away from everything and give him time to deal with things. He hadn't been evasive about the reasons as there was no point, but she readily agreed and looked forward to the visit.

Alfred was relieved. It'd be one less thing for him to worry about. He'd drive her down tomorrow afternoon or maybe get one of the lads to do it. She wasn't so keen on that idea, but they'd left it at him saying "see how it goes" or in other words, lets argue about it later in private.

The rickety glass fronted door opened with some difficulty, and the bell rang.

Tugs moved round to face it and subtly put his hand inside his suit jacket. The lad who came in didn't look like part of a firm, but he was skinny and scruffy with a worried look, which made Tugs nervous.

The lad looked around for a moment and settled his gaze on their table. Tugs got up and motioned the lad to sit at an empty table in front of them, which he did quickly. Tugs sat opposite and fixed his gaze on the boy.

“Mr Kemble?” the boy stuttered.

“I’m his associate.” Tugs answered. “What do you want?”

“I’ve er, got a message from Mr White”. He put his hands flat on the table to show he wasn’t carrying anything. By this time the café had fallen almost silent and all eyes were on them. Tugs looked around and the other customers decided their own breakfasts and conversations might be more interesting. The atmosphere seemed to settle back to what it had been, so he looked back at the youth, who was still in the same position, hands flat on the table and now sweating a little.

Tugs offered him a cigarette and the lad seemed to visibly relax. “Thanks, but I don’t smoke”.

“That’s a good lad” said Tugs. “These things cost a bomb now. Anyway, about this message?”

“Mr White would like to meet Mr Kemble to sort everything out. He’s asked if they can...”

“Which Mr White are we talking about?” Tugs interrupted, “there’s more than one”.

“Oh, er... Harold. Harold White”.

Tugs wasn't surprised. The sensible money was on Harold.

The lad continued. "Mr White. Er. Harold would like to meet somewhere neutral and open with a few people around, for mutual piece of mind."

Tugs was impressed. Either this kid was educated, or he'd learned his lines well. Either way, he wasn't quite the little shit he'd first taken him for.

"What's your name lad?" said Tugs.

"Kevin" replied Kevin.

"Well Kevin, I'll relay the message to Mr Kemble, and someone will be in touch."

Kevin was about to ask how but remembered what he'd been told earlier in The Britannia by Ray, who'd been concerned for his safety. No questions, just deliver the message, listen to what they have to say and leave as soon as possible, but not before you're told. The others in the pub seemed to find it all very funny.

So, he nodded and waited. Tugs motioned towards the door. "Best be on your way then Kevin. Good to meet you." But Tugs didn't extend his hand. After all, this was only a messenger boy.

Kevin left, and Tugs returned to his boss' table. He had a quick glance around as the bell went, just to be certain no one else was coming in.

"It's Harold."

Tugs waited for a reaction but got none, so he continued.

"He wants to meet you. Somewhere public and off the manor."

"What do you think? Sound like a trick?" said Alfred, but he was looking at his wife.

"Harold? Isn't he the nasty little one with the temper?" she answered.

Alfred looked back over at Tugs. "You've met him a few times. What do you think of him?"

Tugs wasn't expecting to be asked his opinion, but he was adept at saying the right things at the right times and thought for a moment before replying.

"He's tough, but Mrs Kemble is right, he has a temper. He can go off at the slightest little thing."

"I'll use the meeting to test that temper of his. See if I can get him angry so he makes a stupid move."

Tugs thought that was a dangerous thing to do, but would never voice it, especially in front of his boss' wife.

Kemble continued, more to himself than anyone else in earshot. "So, Harold's done his own boss in and taken over. There's no loyalty left anymore, especially amongst those Stepney ponces. If he gets half a chance, he'll have me done at the meet, so I want somewhere he can't possibly make any sort of move, and I want him on the back foot. I'll get it set up in the West End, so he'll be as worried about the Maltese as he is about me. But I'm just going to sit and talk, and I might even make a few concessions. Then later that evening, when they're all tucked up at home or in the boozer, we'll hit the fucking lot of them."

Molly sat in silence. She didn't like hearing her husband swearing or talking about murdering people, but that was part of their world and she couldn't always hide away from it.

They continued in silence until the tea was finished and the bill paid. Mick had suggested a tab once but Mr Kemble always preferred to pay up there and then. In all those years he'd never once tipped him or any of the waitresses. But Mick knew someone who'd give him a very decent tip for what he'd just overheard.

*

The meeting between Alfred Kemble and Harold White was arranged for Saturday afternoon at an Italian restaurant in the West End, just off Jermyn Street. The Maltese firms were the main power in that area so would be informed but not involved. And they'd be watched closely in case they tried any moves of their own. Nobody trusted them.

Harold sat with Ray, Henry and Jack in the back room of the Clare Hall discussing the forthcoming meet. They knew Kemble wasn't going to try anything since they got that call earlier from the Café owner, who'd be getting a nice little drink soon. Henry thought it could be false information passed on with the intention of lowering their guard, but the others doubted it. The bloke didn't sound scared or worried, and he wouldn't put his business or family at risk like that, even if Kemble had threatened or paid him to. All the same, they'd still take the necessary precautions.

They decided not to make their own move during the meet. It was far too risky. An innocent passer-by could get hurt, or worse, and there'd be so many witnesses that even the bent coppers would have to put some legwork in, and it wouldn't be long before most of them were taken in for questioning. Then it only took one of them to break and it was all over.

After that, it was just a question of getting to Kemble before his lot got to Harold. There was no realistic chance of any settlement despite anything agreed at the meeting. Harold knew Kemble wanted the East End at whatever cost. It was the springboard to taking control of the West End. And he also knew he wanted it all for himself. Fuck Kemble and any of the others. He'd fight them all if he had to and be the last one standing.

Harold had been on the vodka since he arrived and continued knocking it back at a pace, to the point where even Ray was looking a bit concerned.

He'd been in a good mood when Eric picked him up, but as the journey went on and the conversation died off, he'd started to think about George Patterson, and couldn't erase the image of George's face when his knife went in. Getting smashed was the only way he could think of exorcising what was haunting him.

But even now Harold was well on the way to being pissed, he was still in charge. He got up and walked unsteadily across to the window. The daylight was fading fast and the streets emptying. He looked across to the pale, yellow bricked terraced houses opposite, made brighter by the sunset. They looked much like the houses most of his gang had grown up in and still lived in with their wives and kids. He knocked back the last of the vodka in his glass and turned to face the others, who'd all been watching him staring out of the window, wondering what was going on in his head.

Harold looked at the empty glass in his hand, turning it round as if he could make the contents re-appear by magic. He turned around to face them.

"There's no point in waiting. We wipe him out tomorrow. And the rest of them if they don't fall into line."

This is what they'd waited for. There was no indecision or discussion. It was going to happen and by tomorrow night they'd either rule East London or be lined up next to each other in the morgue.

Jack had a whisper that most of the Wapping firm would be holed up together in a bookies, at least to start with. Kemble didn't want them drinking and this was a clever move in some ways, but stupid in others. Keeping most of his men in the same place was dangerous, especially if Harold could find out where. The problem was there must be at least a dozen bookies on Kemble's patch, and Harold couldn't have his men running around looking in all of them.

They spent the rest of the afternoon making calls and visits, putting out false information to some of Kemble's known grasses, and trying to get as much information as they could. All whilst Harold sat behind his new desk. George's old desk. And continued to knock the vodka back. Henry arranged for Harold to be moved to a safe house in Camden straight after the meeting, and he'd stay to guard him. As for the rest of the plan, they'd need to wait until Harold sobered up tomorrow morning to get the details.

It was dark and late when they eventually left Clare Hall. Henry had to virtually carry Harold home and helped Paula put him to bed. He wondered if she had any idea what he'd done, and why he was acting this way. He was about to leave when Paula called him from the hallway.

"Stay for a quick drink, will you?" she asked.

He pondered on this for a moment then turned back. "Sure, just a quick one though."

She fixed them both a drink and they sat down opposite each other on the low sofa's in the living room. Henry liked the way Paula had done the place out, modern but not too flash. It was how he'd like his place to be if he had someone to share it with.

"He'll be alright won't he Henry? He'll get over this?" Paula asked, probing for an insight into whatever it was he'd done.

Henry looked down at the carpet, unable to meet her gaze. "He's just had a tough couple of days. He'll be fine. Try not to worry about it."

"He's different though. I don't know quite what it is, but he's not been the same since the other night, and he had blood on his hands."

"Come on Paula, it's not like it's the first time he's come home with a few battle scars. It was just a bit of grief."

"Yeah but it's different this time. I just know it. And I can tell you know it too. You've not been able to look me in the eye since you got here."

Henry looked up and met Paula's stare. He thought for a moment about telling her the whole story, about how her husband had stabbed a man to death but thought a slightly alternative version might put an end to the questions. If she felt like she knew something, she might ease off.

"Alright Paula. There's been a lot of grief with Kemble's mob in recent days. We had a run in with some of their boys the other evening in one of the clubs, that's where the blood came from."

Paula listened. Henry paused for a moment before continuing.

"And there's something else. George has gone missing. We don't know what's happened to him, but we can only guess he's been done. Harold's taken over running things for the time being, until we know what's what. That's why he's been acting differently. He's under a lot of pressure."

He hoped she couldn't smell the bullshit.

"You'll look after him, won't you Henry?" was all she said.

Thank Christ for that, he thought. He had to fight hard to disguise the relief running through his body.

But she wasn't fooled for a second. Henry had given her a few facts mixed in with a load of crap. She knew her husband better than most, and she knew when he'd crossed a line. Becoming the guvnor wasn't going to cause him to act this way, not on its own. But she also knew better than to question it further. She'd get nothing more from Henry tonight.

After Henry had finished his drink and left, she couldn't go to bed, not with all the thoughts going around her head, never mind the great snoring lump already in there. There was one consolation, she thought, at least he'd gone past the potentially volatile stage to being virtually comatose before he got home. And she looked forward to his suffering tomorrow morning. Serves him right.

Paula paced around the living room, wearing out the carpet. She wasn't in the mood to drink tea or smoke. She wasn't in the mood for anything, just growing increasingly angry towards her husband. Whatever he'd done, he'd not given a thought for her. Acted like he always did, in his own best interests. So now he was struggling to live with whatever it was. Well, he wasn't the only one. Whatever changes he'd brought on himself also affected her. That was what every bloke who ever joined a firm or committed a crime forgot to consider when they were doing it. It wasn't them who got the shit end of the stick. At worst they'd end up doing a stretch, having their meals cooked and all their needs taken care of, much like they'd done on the outside whilst the wives and girlfriends struggled on without any money, having to do whatever they could to put food on the table and for some of them, clothes on their kids backs. It just wasn't right, wasn't fair. They were like fucking children and we're the idiots who choose to look after them like extensions of their mothers, until the inevitable moment when they let us down. All these years she'd kidded herself Harold wasn't like the rest of them. He was too clever and cared for her too much. Now she just felt like a fool. That's probably what every fucking other wife thought too.

Paula stretched out on the sofa and closed her eyes, willing sleep to come and rescue her from this living nightmare.

Stratford, 1961

It's a lively place and a lot of teds in so there's bound to be trouble later. Still, we might move on in a while. Jack is getting a round in while Ray and me give the place the once over. We're both on the lookout for some decent talent, albeit of a different sort from each other. I just hope he doesn't try to pick up some good-looking ted otherwise we'll end up in a ruck. We're in our best suits, looking sharp and standing out from the crowd. It's a good feeling, knowing you're in a suit that costs more than what most of the others in the place earn in six months.

Jack comes back with the drinks. He's loved up, but I reckon he'd still take a punt if the opportunity came up. So, we stand there for a minute or two just sipping our pints and looking around. I reckon a few people know who we are cos they look away quickly when we meet their stare.

"What do you reckon then Aitch?" says Jack.

I look at him, confused.

"This place" he continues, waving his arm round. "What do you think of it?"

"It's alright" I venture.

"Yeah, it's alright" agrees Ray.

The conversation's always this riveting until we've had a few more beers. But I know we're in for a good night. It's always a good laugh with these two and I don't have to be on my guard, like I am when Henry's out with us.

Ray starts on his favourite subject. Why isn't he part of the firm and can't we put a word in for him? At least he's started early tonight so we can shut him up without him getting too sulky. Jack is doing the honours and I'm losing interest in the conversation, so start gazing around.

Then I see her.

I feel something I've never felt before. A sort of helplessness. I can see her there, but I can't do or say anything. She's clocked me staring over and looks quickly away, back to her mates. But I know she's clocked me.

She's beautiful. Fucking beautiful. Her eyes are amazing and just draw me in. She's wearing a bright green and white dress that finishes just above her knees and has lovely shoulder length brown hair in a sort of bob style that just shimmers. This place doesn't deserve her.

Then I notice her smile and it's directed at me. It takes me a moment to realise but she's looking straight across at me, smiling. Then she pokes her tongue out.

I'm just standing here like a prat, not seeing or hearing anything else. Just staring at this girl. This stunning girl. I suddenly snap out of it, realising what I must look like. Jack's noticed and is looking over at her, then back at me and smiling.

"She's a cracker Aitch" he says, but I'm still barely listening.

"Eh?" is all I can muster in reply.

Jack turns back to Ray. "Look at him." He laughs. "Like a little puppy dog."

Ray laughs too. I'm starting to become a bit of a feature here. All her mates are staring across now as well and I can feel I'm starting to go red, so I turn back to my mates and try to pretend I've been following their conversation all along, but I'm not fooling anyone.

"Go on Harold" says Ray, "Go over and say hello to the poor girl. She's still looking over."

"Yeah, go on." Jack agrees. "Hurry up or some greasy mush with a duck's arse on his head is going to pull her."

That's all I need to hear. I'm not having some fucking ted put his dirty hands on her. I'm not having anyone touch her. I don't know her name, I've not even spoken to her, but want to possess her. So I take a breath and walk over, trying to look calm and relaxed but conscious of the fact she's about the same height as me.

"Hello love. I'm Harold. What's your name?"

She makes me wait for a moment, then looks straight into my eyes. And I'm lost.

Saturday 8th March 1969

Paula brewed up a cuppa and took it through to her husband who was still under the covers and snoring heavily. She shook him roughly awake.

"Thanks love" Harold mumbled in a voice thick with the remnants of the night before, and reached across for the tea, sitting up with a groan. He was not in a good place.

Paula sat on the bed next to him for a moment, watching him in silence while he drank his tea. He wasn't up to having a conversation so was grateful for this. He looked over at her as he finished. "Any chance of another?" he asked.

She took the cup and went back to the kitchen without a word. Harold rose slowly and sat on the end of the bed, looking across and out of the window. It was overcast and might rain at any moment. It suited his current mood and the day ahead. He put his dressing gown on and went to freshen up. When he eventually came into the kitchen, a lukewarm cup of tea was waiting for him on the table, along with a frosty reception.

"How are you feeling?" asked Paula, without a hint of concern.

"Wonderful. How are you?"

She just looked at him.

Harold downed the tea and went back into the bedroom. He didn't have time for this.

He hoped Ray would turn up soon, so he wouldn't have to go back and face more of the same. His prayers were answered as the buzzer went and Paula answered. She buzzed Ray up and made him a coffee while he waited for his new boss to get ready.

Paula watched Ray as he drank his coffee, lounging on the sofa as only he could, with that air of confidence, giving her his easy smile. He wore a tight-fitting black roll-neck, grey pressed trousers and a cream jacket. A bit more somber than usual, she thought, but still a flash sod. She couldn't help noticing the bruising around his eyes and his cut lip and wanted to thank the man who'd given it to him.

Ray noticed her staring and smiled across at her. "How are you then Paula? I like what you've done with the place." He waved his hand around as if to signify his approval of the décor.

She never really knew if he was taking the piss or not. On this occasion, she assumed he wasn't because today wasn't a day to be messing about. But then again, she thought, Ray never took anything completely seriously. She might not have been so certain of that if she'd been there last night while he was tied to a chair in a dingy back room. He'd been taking that very seriously.

"I'm alright thanks. How are you?" She ignored the comment about the décor.

He kept smiling at her. "I'm very well thank you, apart from the bruising. Had a few too many the other night and fell down the stairs. And Harold? How's he feeling this morning?"

Fucking liar, she thought. She smiled back but there was no warmth in it. "As well as can be expected seeing how he drank half of Russia dry last night."

"We did have a few." Ray chuckled. "Mind if I smoke?"

"Help yourself" she replied.

But the way she said it made him think twice. He put the packet back in his jacket pocket. "Maybe later."

They sat in uncomfortable silence for a few minutes before Harold's outline framed the doorway. He was in a grey mohair suit, with trousers finishing wide at the bottom as was the fashion these days. A red patterned tie and crisp white shirt. He might have looked ready, but he didn't feel it. He felt sick.

"We off then?" he said.

Ray got up and looked at Paula. "Thanks for the coffee. See you soon."

Paula said nothing in return. She looked at Harold.

"See you later then love" he said.

"See you."

And that was it. They were out of the door and in the lift. As the doors shut, they both let out a sigh, looked across at each other and laughed, breaking the tension.

"Fuck me. She can be hard work sometimes Ray."

Ray knew to keep a bit of distance where Paula was concerned. After all, she was still his new boss's wife.

"Expect she's a bit worried, that's all. You were in a right state last night. Anyway, big day ahead." Ray smiled. It was that smile only he could give and it reassured Harold.

"Yeah. Big day. You ready?"

The lift reached the ground floor with a jolt and the doors slid back slowly and noisily on their mechanism.

"Ready."

They walked over to Ray's car, Harold going around to the passenger side. Before they got in, Harold looked across at Ray.

"You sure about this Ray? What we talked about last night?"

"You mean you remember that conversation?"

"Come on, don't fuck about. Of course, I remember. I wasn't that pissed."

Ray gave him a look that disagreed with his last statement but didn't push it any further. They'd spoken privately the night before, just before Henry had come over to the bar and literally lifted his brother onto his shoulders. Harold had slurred the plan to him, but it made sense and he could fill in the gaps himself. But Ray was convinced Harold wouldn't remember the conversation this morning. He was wrong, and his best mate continued to surprise him.

"I've got no problem with it, you know that. But some of the others might have."

"Leave them to me. You'll have enough to worry about" Harold replied.

"You know me Aitch, I don't have a care in the world."

You might have after today, thought Harold, as they got into the car.

*

He stood before the full-length mirror in his best brown suit and blue shirt. Alfred placed the tie around his neck and tightened it up, then looked down at his shoes, making out his reflection in them.

He smiled to himself. Today he'd take what was rightfully his. He'd worked too hard and for too long to let some short-arsed, two-bob thug keep it from him. He was much more experienced than his opponent. He wouldn't make it look easy, but he'd let Harold believe he'd got a good deal and put this old man in his place. Then he'd take the necessary steps.

It would have been easier if he'd found out where Harold was going to hole up, but their usually reliable sources had let them down, giving them, all sorts of nonsense. But he still had a plan. If they couldn't cut the head off the snake, they'd chop up the body and the head would die.

One final adjustment of the tie then downstairs where Tugs was waiting in the sitting room, perched awkwardly on one end of the sofa.

He could feel the tension in his bodyguard, but it wasn't a bad thing. He needed to be on his toes today. An attempt on his life at the restaurant, in broad daylight with lots of witnesses was highly unlikely, but you never knew in this game. What he did know was that Tugs would be ready.

"Fit?" he said.

“Ready when you are boss” replied Tugs.

Little was said between them as they left the house, got into the Jaguar and started their journey across London. As they drove slowly through the narrow Limehouse streets Tugs managed a few glances across to his boss, sitting next to him in the passenger seat. There was no emotion, no outward sign of concern. He just sat there, occasionally checking his tie in the mirror and brushing imaginary dust off the lapels of his suit.

Tugs smiled to himself. He’d got the details of their plan over the phone yesterday evening and spent the rest of the night putting it all in place. It was beautiful. Harold and his firm didn’t stand a fucking chance. They’d hit them so quickly and so hard they wouldn’t see it coming, and at the end of it all Harold would be left with nothing.

The fact that little was said gave Tugs even more confidence. If his boss was worried, he wasn’t showing it. He’d not even asked if everything was in place, just took it for granted and didn’t need to go over the same old ground.

The Saturday traffic started to build up as they got towards the West End, but they’d left in plenty of time and would arrive well before the meet started, making sure they got a parking space right outside.

Tugs had his men watching the premises belonging to Harold’s firm, and the Maltese gangs. It spread them around a bit, but they’d soon be on the phone to the restaurant if anyone looked to be doing something suspicious. After the meeting they’d convene back at the bookies in Trinidad Street, and get ready for the main event.

They pulled into Jermyn Street and flashed their lights. The silver car pulled out of the parking space, allowing them to be the first ones in. Once they'd parked up and got out, Caffari shouted across from the open window of the silver car.

"Alright Mr Kemble? All good for you?"

Kemble didn't respond. Tugs gave a thumbs up and the car drove off. Fucking Maltese prick, he thought. Might as well have put a banner up.

*

Henry rolled over and awoke with a start. He'd been in the middle of a bad dream and woken himself up thrashing around. As he came to, he tried to remember what it'd been about, but the images were fading fast. Just something violent. Him going crazy and lashing out at people he knew and people he didn't.

He leant on his elbows and looked at the clock on the wall. In the early morning gloom, he could just about make out the hands telling him it was almost six o'clock. Fuck it. He'd only been asleep for four hours, after his near nightly ritual of giving one to the bird in the flat above while her boyfriend was on the night shift. He'd have to knock it on the head with her soon. Didn't want her getting any ideas. Mind you, after his performance last night he wouldn't be surprised if she knocked it on the head first.

He lay back down and stared at the ceiling. He was soon going to feel crap, but it didn't matter too much as he didn't have a starring role today. He had to be over at the flat by the afternoon and make it ready for when Harold arrived. It felt odd to be working for his brother now, all these years after getting him on to the firm in the first place. Still, he wasn't jealous. He'd never wanted to be the guvnor and didn't begrudge his brother. He didn't even feel angry at the way it had all come about. As much as he liked and respected George, he knew deep down they'd have come under Kemble's thumb sooner rather than later.

Henry didn't lack confidence in his younger brother, but he still worried for him. Either Kemble or Harold would end up ruling the East End and the other one would end up dead. He'd wanted to act as bodyguard at the meeting, but Kemble wouldn't accept it. It was just like that slimy little arsehole to stir things up and make pointless demands.

Now it was down to Ray to keep his brother safe, and that too worried Henry. Ray could take care of himself, but he wasn't in the same league as Tugs. If something went wrong, he knew who his money would be on.

He continued to lay and stare and think until he eventually dropped off to sleep, waking again at twenty past ten and feeling slightly better. He'd fix himself some breakfast and take a leisurely drive over to Camden, making sure he wasn't followed. He was in the bathroom when the phone went. He rushed to pick it up and heard the pips go. Harold's voice came on the other end of the line.

"Henry?"

"Harold? Where are you? What's wrong?"

"Don't worry, nothing's wrong. We're on our way over to the meet. I just need to tell you something."

Either his brother had suddenly developed a sensitive side and was calling to tell him what a wonderful sibling he was, or their plans had changed.

Harold continued. "Me and Ray have sorted out how we're going to get to Kemble. It won't be easy and none of the chaps know about it. I just wanted to put you in the picture."

"Harold, don't do anything at the meet or we're finished."

"Don't be silly. I'm not going to shoot anyone in the middle of the West End. I haven't got long. I just wanted to let you know that I'll be arriving alone later. Ray will have to go away for a while."

"What are you going to do?"

"I can't tell you right now. I'm going to run out of coins in a minute and I need to get going. Get the flat ready then get over to Acer Road in Dalston. I'll meet you there."

"Acer Road? Now wait Harold..." Henry started to say, but the pips went again, and he knew Harold wouldn't be calling back. Henry slammed the phone down and paced the hallway. What were they thinking of, taking unnecessary risks? If he'd been involved this would never have happened, but that was what burned in him. He hadn't been involved. He'd been sidelined, reduced to a fucking housemaid and taxi driver.

Fucking Ray, he thought. He's going to get us all killed.

*

Harold followed Ray into the large and tackily decorated Italian restaurant. They looked around for a moment or two before spotting Kemble sitting alone at a table for four by the back wall. They gave their coats to the waitress and made their way over. Kemble watched them all the way. When they got to the table there was no handshake and little acknowledgement from either side as they sat down.

“On your own?” asked Harold, knowing perfectly well it wasn’t the case.

Kemble looked across towards the toilet. Harold exchanged a quick concerned glance with Ray. Kemble clocked this and gave them his snake-like smile. It was just the reaction he wanted. First blood to him.

They sat in silence for a few minutes. Kemble had taken the seats that looked towards the door and Harold felt vulnerable. He looked around the place. It was done out in mostly green and white, with a bit of red thrown in here and there. A large Italian flag adorned one wall as if anyone really needed a reminder. The large glass windows at the front made it light and airy throughout, which was a rare nice touch amongst the worn furniture and plastic plants. It was too early for the tourists so only a few other tables were occupied. None of the other patrons looked all that suspicious but you could never tell. Harold was beginning to think coming here had been a mistake and his nervousness wasn’t helped by the waitress appearing out of nowhere to take their drink orders. Harold ordered a whisky and water and Ray chose to have an orange juice.

Kemble ordered two lime and sodas. As the waitress left, Tugs appeared and sat down next to his boss. Harold nodded and got the same in return. The menus stayed flat on the table.

They continued sitting there in total silence for a few minutes until the drinks appeared. Harold could see they'd clocked the state of Ray's face but neither mentioned it. Eventually, Kemble spoke.

"It's very good of you to meet me Harold. Especially in such difficult circumstances."

"These things happen Alfred" replied Harold, keen to move things on.

Harold knew they'd all notice his use of Kemble's first name. He was the equal of this man and wouldn't be deferential. He also knew it'd get right up his hooter.

"They do, they do" Kemble agreed. "Well now it's done, and we need to get everything back to normal, for everybody's sake. I think we can work out a mutually beneficial arrangement today. I'm more than happy to let things stay as they are between us, with a few small adjustments."

"What small adjustments?" Harold asked.

Kemble seemed keen to play this down. He leant forward slightly. "Nothing significant Harold. Before they went down, the twins had promised me one or two things George was reluctant to part with. It was all in the process of being sorted out but with the trial and everything, it probably slipped their minds."

Harold paused. He didn't want to make this seem too easy.

"We'll the twins aren't here to confirm anything are they? We should order. I'm starving."

Harold could see Kemble and Tugs had been taken off guard by the change in tack. He knew he'd got the upper hand for the time being, but things could change again very quickly. They studied the menus for a few minutes and when they'd all placed them back down, the waitress was across in seconds. She'd been keeping a close eye on this group, watching their body language. She'd come to the conclusion that they seemed to be here to make some sort of business deal but didn't really like each other much. Whatever this was all about, she had the feeling there might be a decent tip.

They ordered unimaginatively. The waitress left, and they sat in silence again. Ray and Tugs nursed their drinks and said nothing, waiting for their bosses to resume fencing. This time it was Harold who broke the silence.

"So, what were you were promised?"

"Nothing important Harold. A couple of bookies on your side of the fence, that's all. Oh, and Clare Hall."

Ray looked across at Harold, but still said nothing.

"Clare Hall is a major earner for us. You know that" said Harold.

"It was once, but I hear it's a bit run down these days."

"Not been there lately?" Harold goaded.

"Let's not get ahead of ourselves" replied Kemble. He appeared to be thinking. "Alright then Harold, you can keep Clare Hall, but I want some compensation. Something decent."

It was Harold's turn to look like he was considering. He investigated his nearly empty glass for a moment or two. "How about the George Tavern? That's a reasonable earner."

Kemble had expected a flat refusal, but in some ways, this was worse. The George Tavern was more trouble than it was worth. A few local drunks in at lunchtime and a guaranteed punch up in the evening. Even so, he gave the appearance of giving it serious thought. Eventually he spoke.

"I'm sorry Harold. That's not going to work for me. I tell you what. You give me the bookies I'd been promised and thirty percent share in Clare Hall, and we've got a deal."

I'll give you a fucking deal, thought Harold. I'll wipe that slimy grin off your face in a minute. He could feel himself getting angry but knew this was what Kemble wanted. What he kept prodding him for. He quickly pushed it back down but couldn't entirely hide what he was feeling.

"Thirty percent? No chance. Why should I give you anything?"

"You don't have to give me anything at all Harold" Kemble replied, calmly. "I understand any deal I had with the twins was before you took over, but it'd be a gesture of good faith and I'm sure over time we could learn to trust each other."

Harold knew this was Kemble's game, and he'd started playing along with it. Inside, he was boiling but knew he needed to keep things calm, otherwise his plan had no chance of succeeding. "Alright" he said, "Ten percent of the Clare, and the bookies."

Kemble smiled again. "Ten percent hardly seems worth bothering with. Twenty percent is a reasonable amount. How about twenty?"

"Alright then" Harold replied, too quickly, "Twenty it is. And everything else stays as it is." He cursed himself for coming over so keen. But it was too late, and anyway it was all going to be meaningless in a few hours.

"Good" said Kemble. "I'm glad that's sorted. It's in our interests to keep South London and the rest of them away. If we're tearing each other apart, they'll just take what's left over."

Harold couldn't disagree with that, but a war of attrition wasn't the plan. Once the main business was out of the way they chatted awkwardly about possible threats from other parts of the city and what had happened to the twins before their meals arrived.

They ate quickly and silently. Preferring to concentrate on the food and declining deserts and coffees. Harold didn't want to spend any more time in the company of Alfred Kemble than was necessary and the feeling was mutual. As they sat with the bill on the table between them, Alfred extended his hand to Harold.

"So, we're agreed?"

Harold took his clammy hand and shook it firmly. "Agreed" he replied.

The waitress had been right about this little group. Tugs and Ray split the cost of the meal and both put in a hefty tip, not wanting to be outdone. After they'd left, she was over like a shot and counted it up. It came to just over a week's wages. Bollocks was she sharing this one out with the rest of them.

They left the restaurant and went their separate ways without goodbyes. Harold and his right-hand man were almost back on home territory when Ray parked down a Dalston side street. They sat and waited for a few minutes, but nothing followed them.

"You sure about this Ray?" asked Harold. "It's a big risk. You could be wrong."

"Yeah, I could be. If he's not there we keep looking, but if I'm right, and he's there, we can finish this quickly."

"What if he's tooled up, or got people with him?"

Ray laughed. "Come on Harold, you know me by now. I'm not going in there all guns blazing. I'll see how the land lies. But if he's on his own I'll top him, tooled up or not."

Harold smiled. He trusted this man like no other. After what they'd been through over the years, and watching him take that beating, he felt a familiar surge of affection. Ray had accepted him as his boss without question or complaint and now he was putting his life on the line for him, again.

Harold shook Ray's hand and got out of the car. He walked a little way up the road and got into another waiting car, with his brother Henry behind the wheel. They pulled away and headed towards Camden.

Ray waited until they'd got to the turning before he pulled away. He was on a different journey. It was a gamble and could be the last one he ever took.

As he drove, he thought back over the events of the last few days. He couldn't believe he was still alive. It was only Harold's force of will that stopped Henry putting him in the hospital or worse. He knew Henry didn't like him and didn't need much of an excuse to give him a beating.

Even if his new boss didn't realise it, Ray owed his life to him. Deep down, he knew he'd not have lasted five minutes in charge. They wouldn't have accepted him, and the challenges would have come quickly, if Kemble hadn't got to him first. He knew this was the best outcome all round. Harold was feared and respected. A natural leader. Of course, he had his faults but even these could be put to good use if the occasion suited. After all, a bit of unpredictability came in handy.

Ray turned the car south towards the Rotherhithe Tunnel. Harold was right, this was a big risk. It could turn out to be a wild goose chase or the end of all their problems, so it was a risk worth taking.

*

Alfred Kemble stood in the hallway of his sister-in-law's house in Sittingbourne, using her telephone and staring disapprovingly at the awful wallpaper.

"It doesn't matter if no one knows where he is. We go as planned at eight o'clock. If he doesn't have an army, he can't fight a war, can he?"

He was agitated and speaking in hushed tones. Molly and her sister, Maisy were just through in the living room. And Maisy would be all fucking ears.

"It happens quickly and as quietly as possible. We won't have any problems from the law if there's not much mess. Once we take them out, he's finished. I'll call later, when it's done."

He put the phone down, still agitated but confident Tugs would take care of things properly.

His plan was set. Tugs and the rest of his top boys would take out Eric, Ray, Jack and Henry, even if it had to be in their homes. Losing four top lieutenants would cripple Harold's gang and the rest would fall into line. Harold himself would be finished, and the East End would finally belong to him. If he needed to break the rules on this one occasion, then so be it. It didn't occur to him that Harold might be thinking along the same lines.

Going over the plan again had made him feel better, and ready to return to the chintzy, flowery living room where Molly and Maisy were perched on the sofa, both looking expectantly at him as he entered, as if he was going to tell them all about his plans for Harold and his pals.

"I'm sorry about that, just a little bit of business. All done now. Any more tea in the pot?"

He finished his tea and quickly tired of the conversation. Despite the mental torture he knew he had to sit it out and just wait. They'd be safe to return home tomorrow and he'd make sure Tugs came to pick them up early. Until then he knew he just had to tolerate it, even if it was a fate worse than death.

For the time being though, he could do with a breather. He knew how the evening would play out. The tea would be replaced by Gin and Maisy would start on about Ted, and how he'd left her for that trollop at the office. Although it wasn't the done thing, he had some sympathy with the man, and Maisy hadn't done too badly out of the divorce, keeping this place and a tidy portion of Ted's income. He stood up and politely announced he was off outside for a cigarette.

When he'd left the room, he could hear them talking about what a lovely man he was. He smiled wryly to himself and made his way through the small kitchen at the back and into the garden. He stood on the patio in the warm, quiet evening. The lawn was well maintained and the borders full of flowers he'd never heard of. It was the sort of garden he'd like for Molly, but she wasn't green fingered like her sister and he didn't have time for all that. Not for a few more years anyway.

After a few minutes, he took out a fag and lit up. He was relieved to be away from the constant discussion about home furnishings and the goings-on of the neighbours. He'd savor these minutes.

*

From a gap between the door and the frame inside the shed at the end of the garden, Ray watched Alfred Kemble smoking. This was a stroke of luck he hadn't expected and an opportunity he couldn't waste. At least this way he wouldn't have to do it in front of those women. He might have been tempted to put one in each of them as well. He fixed the silencer to the end of the pistol and puled the balaclava down.

Harold had been concerned about taking Kemble out in these circumstances, but it was too late for all that now. The time had come, and Ray knew it was the only way they could win this without all-out war. Momentarily he felt uncomfortable about the women having to find the body, but they'd get over it, eventually.

He was snapped out of his thoughts by the sight of his target dropping his cigarette on the floor and stubbing it out. He saw Kemble turn towards the kitchen door. Ray opened the shed door and Kemble immediately looked back to see where the noise had come from. Ray strode quickly and purposefully across the manicured lawn and pumped two shots into the stunned, frozen figure of Alfred Kemble. By the time he reached the patio, the man was on his knees, desperately clawing at the wounds in his chest and shoulder, as if he could pull the bullets out.

Kemble looked up. Ray didn't say anything. Didn't hesitate. One more bullet straight between the eyes. The lifeless body fell backwards, his knees sticking up awkwardly. Blood began to pool on the patio. As the evening drew in on a suburban street in Kent, Alfred Kemble died.

Ray was over the fence, into the garden next door, through the gate and out into the alleyway. He quickly removed the balaclava and stuffed that and the pistol inside his jacket.

He got to the end of the alleyway and looked towards the street. There were a couple of kids playing with a ball a bit further down, but they wouldn't get a good look at him, and wouldn't be considered reliable witnesses anyway. He strode quickly to the car and pulled away as quietly as possible. He was gone before screams filled the quiet air.

*

The men were getting fidgety and bored, cramped up in the back room of the bookies. They'd played cards for the past couple of hours but now just sat around. The room wasn't exactly palatial and had started to smell of sweat and stale farts.

Kemble had left instruction. The targets were to be picked up and dealt with at eight o clock. Tugs wouldn't let them leave before half seven. He insisted on running through the plans with each one of them, over and again. This was done to figure out if any of them were having second thoughts.

They were to pick their targets up from their homes or wherever they'd gone to, drive them somewhere quiet and take care of things. If they met any resistance then it had to happen straight away, even if it meant doing it in front of their mates or families. It wasn't the way anyone wanted it to go, but too much was riding on tonight, and the mess could be sorted out later if necessary.

The only one Tugs wasn't worried about was Eddie Fuller. Eddie was a natural when it came to this sort of thing. He'd had a fair bit of practice if the stories were to be believed, and could make it happen quickly, quietly and pretty much painlessly. Tugs smiled to himself at the phrase Eddie coined for it, giving them an OBE, or 'one behind the ear'.

The phone rang, and they all turned towards it. It was only just gone seven, too early for another call from his boss unless something was wrong or needed to be changed. Tugs felt several pairs of eyes watching him. He reached over to answer, praying it was just some information about the whereabouts of their targets.

"Yeah?"

"Your boss is dead, so whatever you had planned, call it off."

"Who's this?" said Tugs. He thought he recognised the voice as Jack's.

"I've told you; Alfred Kemble is dead. Don't try anything silly. We'll be waiting."

"Is that you Jack? Are you taking the piss?" They could see the fury spreading across Tugs' face as they listened to his side of the call.

"I'm not saying it again. If you don't believe me take a drive down to Kent and have a look for yourself. They'll be putting what's left of him in the back of a van about now."

"You cunt!" Tugs exploded. "I'll fucking bury you. I'll kill the fucking lot of you!"

Before he'd finished his tirade, the line had gone dead.

They were all looking at him as he threw the receiver to the floor, taking the cradle down with it. His reaction told them all they needed to know.

After a couple of moments, in difficult silence whilst Tugs brooded, Bob 'Geordie' Mackenzie was the first to speak up.

"So, it's off then?"

"No, it fucking well isn't" Tugs shot back. "It's fucking war. They killed him at his sister-in-law's place. For Christ's sake, that's unforgiveable".

Even as he said it, he knew they weren't convinced. After all, they'd planned to do something similar. And these were working men with families to provide for, and codes of honour only went so far. But Tugs wasn't going to be denied even if it meant going it alone. He grabbed a gun off the table and stormed towards the door. No one tried to stop him. As the door slammed behind him, the rest of the men looked towards Geordie for their own instructions.

"Go home. Leave the tools here, I'll sort it out." He said.

"What about Tugs?" asked one of the newer additions that Geordie didn't really know too well.

"He'll go after one of the Stepney lot or run around until he's picked up by the law. There's nothing we can do about it now, so go home and I'll speak to Jack or one of the others tomorrow and get things squared off. You'll be okay, just keep your head down and have an early night."

This seemed to satisfy them, and they slowly gathered up their things and began shuffling out. They'd been prepared to carry out their bosses plans but he was no longer around, and Stepney had the upper hand. None of them wanted to carry on and get banged up or killed. They had confidence in Geordie to sort something out, so they could get back to earning as quickly as possible.

After they'd gone, Geordie quietly packed up the weapons in worn out army surplus bags and placed them under the floorboards. He replaced the rug and table and sat down, poured himself a drink and stretched out. He needed to think and relax for a moment. He'd worry about moving the guns tomorrow. Right now, he was more concerned with sorting things out with Stepney, and as quickly as possible. He owed it to the rest of the lads and hoped Harold would be reasonable and take most of them on.

He finished his scotch, picked the phone up off the floor and checked it still worked. He got the dialing tone and dialed the number for the Clare Hall. A voice came on the other end of the line.

"Hello, Clare Hall."

"Is Jack there?"

"Who's this?"

"It's Geordie."

There was a silence that lasted a few minutes, then another voice came on the line.

"Alright Geordie? It's Jack".

"Alright Jack. We got the message and it's over. The lads have all gone home."

"That's good news."

"One problem though" said Geordie, "Tugs, he's gone on the rampage".

"Oh, for fuck's sake. Is he tooled up?"

"Yeah"

"Who's he gone after? Does he know where Harold is?"

"No, no one does. I don't know who he's after, but if he can't find Harold, I'd guess it's probably Ray."

"He won't find him either. Alright, let me know if you hear anything else or if he gets in touch. I'll put the word out to the lads."

"Will do" confirmed Geordie.

"Cheers for the warning. It's a fucking relief it didn't come to a shootout. Come over the Britannia tomorrow night for a drink and we'll get everything straightened out."

After Geordie had put the phone down, he poured himself another drink and thought about Tugs. They'd been good mates over the years, and he was surprised how bad he'd taken the news. It was just one of those things. Okay, it was a bit out of order topping the bloke in front of his missus, but these were strange times and was it really all that different to what they'd have done to one of Harold's boys if they'd put up a fight? Now Tugs was on the loose with a shooter and it could really jeapoardise the situation if he managed to off somebody. Maybe he should have tried to stop him but that wouldn't have been a wise move.

He hoped that Tugs would maybe chase around for a while and come back with his tail between his legs. Either that, or, and hated himself for thinking it, that he'd end up arrested or dead before he could do any serious damage.

Geordie looked at the empty glass in front of him, and the dregs in the bottle on the table and realised he should take his own advice, get home and get his head down. He picked up his jacket and headed out of the door, switching off the lights and locking up. It looked like his new boss was going to be Harold White, and the thought of that pleased him. He'd always got on well with Harold, and personally he thought having some new blood would be a good thing. The time had come for change.

He shrugged his jacket on and started the short stroll to the bus stop, whistling to himself.

*

Tugs was getting into the motor when he felt a tap on his shoulder. He spun around, ready to smash his fist into whoever it was. Eddie Fuller stood behind him, and he thought better of it.

"Not back in there counting Harold's money with your mates?" said Tugs.

If Eddie was annoyed by this comment, he didn't show it. "Where are you off to then?" he asked.

"What the fuck's it got to do with you? How do I know you won't go straight back in there and get on the blower to Stepney?"

It was a stupid thing to say to a man like Eddie Fuller. Tugs knew and regretted saying it. Eddie wasn't a working man like the others, he was a gangster through and through, and a killer. You didn't piss off a killer if you could help it.

Now it was Eddie's turn to be annoyed. "What do you take me for? Some sort of grass? You can stick it up your arse then."

Tugs sighed. "Look, I'm sorry Eddie. I'm just fucking steaming about all this. It's well out of order, gunning him down like that. In cold blood, in front of his wife."

This was music to Eddie's ears. Personally, he didn't give a fuck about all that code of honour nonsense. For all he cared, they could have killed Kemble in front of his wife, his mum and the local vicar. He wanted to get involved but not for the reasons Tugs probably thought he did. Not for revenge, but purely and simply because he enjoyed killing, and he'd been looking forward to tonight. He needed to keep his hand in, and the opportunity to do someone wasn't going to elude him that easily.

"Where are you going then?" Eddie asked again.

"I'm going after Harold. He has to come back home at some point and when he does, I'll be waiting" replied Tugs.

"Want a hand?"

"You can look for Ray if you want. If he was the one that did Alfred he'll be on his toes, but he might go back to his gaff first. And if you find that fucking poof, make it a slow and painful end."

Eddie smiled.

*

It was dark outside, and the rain pattered gently against the window of Chief Inspector Reynolds' office. The only light in the room came from a small desk lamp and the blurred yellow street lights outside. The Chief Inspector sat behind his desk in his immaculate uniform, waiting impatiently for the arrival of the man he'd summoned over fifteen minutes ago. He didn't like being kept waiting, especially when he knew the person concerned was just delaying the inevitable.

Eventually there was a knock at the door.

"Come".

DS Lewis entered.

"Sit down Detective Sergeant." ordered the Chief Inspector. Lewis sat down at the desk, opposite his superior.

"Quiet night?" he continued.

"Nothing out of the ordinary so far, Sir." Lewis replied in all innocence, though he knew it was a leading question.

"Well something very out of the ordinary occurred in Kent earlier this evening. Chief Inspector Hagan phoned me half an hour ago. A gangland execution."

Lewis decided to continue playing dumb. "Kent Sir? That's quite far out of our jurisdiction."

Reynolds was becoming irritated by the feigned ignorance of his subordinate. “Yes, it is. But the victim is usually well within our jurisdiction”.

Lewis dropped the act. “I assume it was someone known to us Sir.”

“Someone very well known to us. Alfred Kemble was shot dead earlier this evening at his sister-in-law’s place in Sittingbourne. Hagan’s less than happy about his men having to deal with a dead London gangster and a hysterical woman. As I’m sure you appreciate, this isn’t a welcome turn of events for him, or for us.”

Lewis wasn’t surprised in the slightest but tried to look as though he was. “His wife was with him then?”

“Yes, she was, but Molly Kemble is taking everything rather calmly. It’s her sister who’s hysterical. Understandable really, after discovering her brother-in-law with his brains splattered all over her nice patio.”

Reynolds was aware of the attempt to divert his attention towards trivial matters. He brushed it aside and continued.

“We have a lot to deal with, Detective Sergeant. That’s two gang bosses either dead or missing two days since the Krays were put away. Whilst we’re busy congratulating ourselves and telling the general public of London we’ve made their streets safer, there’s a gang war erupting in front of us, and as I’m led to understand, not a single arrest. Not so much as a parking ticket.”

Reynolds voice had risen to the point where those in the surrounding offices had stopped what they'd been doing and started listening. He continued at the same volume.

"As you can imagine, those on the floors above us are not happy. Not happy at all. So, I receive a kicking and in turn dish out a kicking to those below me, starting with you."

"With respect Sir, there's always trouble when the market opens up like this" replied Lewis, who was well used to the occasional kicking. "We expected some in-fighting before it all settles down". In the ensuing silence, Lewis looked over enviously at his Chief Inspectors well stocked drinks cabinet but there was as much chance of being offered a glass of something as there was of Cilla Black bursting in and dancing on the desk. His superior's angry response snapped Lewis out of his little daydream.

"In that case what are you and your men doing about it? If you expected problems, you should have been ready for them. As I see it, we're being led a merry dance by Harold White and his associates, and that leads me to one of two possible conclusions. The one I'm settling on for now, is that you're two steps behind and need to catch up. Quickly. This carnage needs to stop, and if it doesn't, I'm going to start thinking of the other possible conclusion for your lack of results, and that is something you really don't want."

"I'll pay him a visit tomorrow morning sir" replied Lewis. The message had been received and understood. He would be visiting Harold in any case, when he resurfaced. But Lewis knew the fight was already as good as over and Harold had taken control of East London quickly and decisively. The only surprise for him was how little bloodshed there'd been. He wondered to himself what Reynolds and those other brass buttons on the top floor had expected? A bunch of gangsters having a nice chat and settling things amicably over a cup of tea? They really needed to get out of their offices occasionally and start walking around the dirty streets.

Reynolds has quietened down now, much to the disappointment of those craning their necks to hear outside and continued a little more cordially. "I appreciate you've had a lot to deal with since DI Thompson went sick, but you need to get a handle on this situation Detective Sergeant. I don't want any further dead bodies or missing persons, even if it is from the criminal fraternity. That's all for now."

"Leave it with me, Sir".

Lewis left the darkened office and sauntered down the corridor back to his own desk, ignoring the inquisitive gazes. Ever one for an eye on the main chance, he'd already been planning a visit to negotiate a mutually beneficial arrangement with Harold. Now he could make it look like his direct intervention had put a stop to the killings. If things played out how he expected them to, it might even mean a permanent promotion.

He was smiling to himself when he picked up the phone and dialed down to the main desk. The voice of young Constable Davis came on the line.

"Yes Sir?"

"Davis, if anything's reported in about the Stepney or Wapping firms, I need to know straight away. Is that clear?"

"Yes Sir."

"Make sure it comes to me directly. There's an ongoing operation so I need total discretion from you." It always helped to make them feel like they were part of some secret operation.

"I'll make sure anything goes to you straight away Sir."

Lewis knew the lad would be as good as his word. Davis wasn't the most astute of the recent intake, but the boy followed orders. He took out his fags and lit one up, leaning back on his chair and looking at his watch as he exhaled the first drag. He was on duty all night and had time to kill so grabbed his coat and radio and went straight down the pub. They'd know exactly where to find him.

*

The Camden flat belonged to a cousin of Eric's. It was a bit shabby, as you'd expect in this area, but reasonably well furnished and stocked with a few bottles in advance of Harold's visit. The cousin was well compensated with a decent West End hotel room and a bit of company for the night.

Henry had taken the call from Ray and relayed the message to his brother. It was done, and they'd have to hope it was accepted across the manor. A further call from Jack shortly afterwards shattered that hope.

Jack had acted quickly, putting the word around to all the chaps about Tugs and sorting them out with weapons. Harold would see him right for a few quid, but he had other priorities right now. It was arguable whether they'd violated some code or other by topping Kemble at his sister-in-law's, and Tugs obviously thought they had, although his anger it was probably more out of loyalty to his boss than any perceived injustice.

Harold felt his brother looking at him as soon as he'd put the phone down, having got the gist of the message from hearing half the conversation.

"Tugs has gone off then?" said Henry. "Anyone else with him?"

"Nah" replied Harold. "Just Tugs. All the rest of the firm are happy to go home and report for work as normal tomorrow."

"What about Eddie Fuller?" said Henry, looking worried.

"He's not part of the firm. He's probably buggered off to South London or somewhere, now there's not going to be a war."

"What do you think Tugs is going to do?" asked Henry.

"He'll be coming after me of course" said Harold.

"And when he doesn't find you?"

"Ray?" said Harold. "He won't find him either."

"We need to get Paula some protection" said Henry.

It'd annoyed Harold that his brother considered this first. He felt a bit embarrassed he'd mentioned Ray before his own wife. And suddenly he was extremely worried for her. The thought hadn't entered his head that they'd do anything to the families, but the rules were changing.

"Yeah, I'll give her a call" he said.

"She's best off staying where she is Harold. We don't want her wandering around the streets. I can be there in twenty minutes. Give her a bell now and tell her I'll be there soon. And try not to worry her."

"Try not to worry her? Fucking Hell Henry, she's worried enough as it is. Get going then."

After his brother had left, he called his wife and gave her the message. The conversation was curt on both sides and that suited him. It wasn't the time for arguments or discussion.

Now Harold sat on the sofa watching a late-night chat show. The presenter was gushing over some American actor, but Harold wasn't taking it in. He finished his scotch and picked up the bottle for a refill. It was three quarters empty, but he was too wound up to feel the full effect.

Henry had called when he got to Paula, just to let him know she was safe. Harold felt much better knowing his brother was there with her, but he couldn't relax until they had Tugs out of the way. Then he could start making plans and thinking of the future.

Harold refilled his glass, got up and walked over to the window. He pulled the faded curtain back and looked out on the empty streets of Camden Town. Rubbish littered the pavement and the street lights were even weaker here than in Stepney. He drew the curtains and went back to the sofa. He didn't like being off his manor, and even less being in this North London shit-hole. Gentle applause accompanied the credits now rolling on the chat show and the channel would be closing down soon. He gulped the scotch and lay back on the sofa. He knew the only way a dreamless sleep would come was to drink himself into oblivion.

*

Henry parked up as near to the flats as he could and waited for a moment. He got out and looked around at the other parked cars. Nothing struck him as out of the ordinary, so he walked over and buzzed the flat. After a moment Paula's voice came on the intercom and she let him up.

He checked behind him to make sure the doors shut, and no one was following. He double locked the flat door when he got up there and went through to the living room where Paula was sitting, watching the television. He could see she was scared.

She didn't turn to look at him but forced a smile.

"There's tea in the pot. Help yourself."

"Thanks" he replied. "Want another?"

"Not for me. I'll be up pissing all night" she said, and they both laughed, the tension broken.

Whilst he was pouring his tea, Henry thought it was strange that Paula hadn't asked after Harold. He took his tea into the hallway and dialed the number on the scrap of paper, giving Harold the message that he'd arrived, and all was well. He thought his brother sounded halfway pissed, and that wasn't an altogether bad thing.

Henry went back through to the living room. The television was off now, and Paula seemed to have relaxed a bit but was still unable to meet his eyes.

"He's alright Paula. He's safe and I reckon he'll be back tomorrow."

Paula looked up. Her eyes were red, but dry. If she'd been crying, she'd stopped a long while ago. "Is this my life now Henry?" she asked, and the tears started to well again.

He sat down beside her, placing his tea on the low table and put his arm around her, letting her head fall onto his chest and the mascara mark his crisp white shirt.

"It's just for tonight love" he said. "Harold's sorted everything out. He just needs to let the dust settle and things will be back to normal, you'll see." He lifted her head and smiled at her. It wouldn't do to tell her about a thug on the rampage, after Harold's blood. Or anyone's blood for that matter.

Paula let her head fall back onto his chest. "I don't know if I can deal with this anymore." she said. "He's changed. Over the past few days things have changed for both of us."

"What do you mean?" Henry asked. "You're not...?" his voice trailed away.

"Oh, I don't know what I mean. My mind's going in a hundred different directions. I'm not stupid Henry. I know he's not a travelling salesman and I've accepted a lot over the years but all I'm hearing about lately is people going missing, being killed or going to prison."

Henry looked straight ahead. He'd always underestimated Paula. She was a lot stronger than he'd thought but even he had to admit things were getting dangerous for them all. The rewards were greater now, but so was everything else that came with it. The jealousy, greed and mistrust they'd have to deal with now. And there was the immediate problem facing them. The one he couldn't bring himself to tell her about.

Whilst they sat in silence, Paula thought too. She was the boss's wife now and didn't know whether to feel elated or petrified. After all, look what was happening to the old bosses, all going to prison or being murdered. Is that how it was going to be for her husband in five or ten years, or sooner? Why couldn't Henry or one of the others become the boss? She didn't care who as long as it wasn't her husband. All the money, jewelry and expensive clothes were worth fuck all in the end.

Paula knew Henry was watching her, trying to figure out what was going on in her mind. She knew he hadn't held her in very high regard, but she wasn't going to let him see her scared. She was a strong woman and right now, if Harold was going to come through all this, she needed to be strong for him. Whether she could put up with all that came from being the boss's wife would have to wait for another time.

She sat upright, moving away from his embrace but staying close to him. He could sense the change in her as she spoke again.

"We'll be fine Henry. I want to help you and help Harold. If there's anything you need me to do just say."

"You can get me another cup of tea if you want?" said Henry.

“Piss off. Get it yourself and make me one while you’re out there” she replied, smiling again.

*

Anthony Elroy Barrett, or Tugs to those who knew him, sat in his car at the far end of the estate. He'd parked up about half an hour ago. A bloke sitting in a car for that long got a few curtains twitching and he was a bit concerned. If the old bill were called and found him sitting here with a gun in his pocket, they wouldn't be especially lenient. Fucking hell, they'd nick him just for being black and it wouldn't be the first time either.

Born to a white woman from Wapping after a dalliance with a Jamaican sailor towards the end of the war, she'd had a tough time of it. Shunned by her neighbours, they'd got looks and comments wherever they went. But she loved him just as much as any other East End mother would do for their own, white son. More so in fact. He'd never know his father and she knew what was coming for him when he got older. She readied him for everything. The comments, the name-calling and the fights. Since he was old enough to understand she'd told him he was different, and people would hate him for it. For no reason, other than that. But she also told him he was special and taught him to be proud of who he was, and where he came from.

And he was. He'd grown up tall, strong and athletic. He guessed it was from his father's side but would never know. The kids in his school soon learned they could call him all the names they wanted to, but if they tried to take him on, they'd end up getting the worst of it.

One day the inevitable happened. A teacher's wallet had been stolen and the finger was naturally pointed at him. He hadn't been anywhere near and didn't know who'd done it. But that didn't seem to matter. He was blamed, found guilty without any evidence and expelled.

When he witnessed his mum laying into the Headmaster that afternoon, first verbally then physically, he never loved anyone as much as in that moment. He knew that whatever happened, there was one person who'd always be in his corner.

On his street he was just one of the gang. Maybe they liked having him around because he could handle himself. But it was something more. They didn't care what colour he was, or whether his Dad was around. To them, he was just Tone, and eventually, for reasons he'd long forgotten, Tugs. The little group went everywhere and did everything together, messing about at the local picture hall and eventually, when they were a bit older, sneaking into the docks to thieve.

It was the only time he really felt he'd let his mum down. They got a bit too successful and eventually some dockers caught up with them. He bore the brunt of their anger. Lifting stuff was their game, and they weren't going to have some local urchins ruining things. He'd taken a beating that night but although he didn't realise at the time, it'd been the making of him. Because he gave as good as he got, and it took three big dockers to eventually get the better of him. He could dish it out and take it with the best of them and it brought him to the attention of Alfred Kemble who'd taken him on, taken him under his wing and made him the man he was today.

It had been a strange relationship, not really a father figure but a bond had developed between the old white gangster and his mixed-race charge. What was also strange was that not once did Alfred mention his background. It seemed totally inconsequential to him and if anyone in the gang made comments they were dealt with swiftly. Usually just a look from Kemble would do the trick. As a result, he'd grown to have total respect for his boss. And total loyalty, even now after his death.

He'd drifted off a little bit and didn't quite see the man who got out of the car and went to the entrance. Was it Harold? It looked a bit like him, but he couldn't be sure. Bollocks. He should have stayed alert.

He'd calmed down a little after leaving the betting shop. The drive over to Stepney had cooled his blood, but he was still going to take his revenge. He doubted it would stop his firm being taken over, but he'd never work for that short-arsed bastard in any case. He was going to have his head.

Surely Harold wouldn't be stupid enough to come back straight away and would send one of his goons instead. It was hard to tell in the darkness, but it did look a lot like him. Tugs' plan had been to get information from the unfortunate individual before topping them, then pay Mr White a visit. Despite his burning sense of injustice at the way they'd dealt with his boss, he wouldn't touch the man's wife. That wasn't his style. Now he was in luck. Could it really be the man himself?

He gave it a few minutes and walked over to the doorway. It was locked but could be opened from within. He wondered whether to buzz another flat and pretend to be a pissed up neighbour, but it was a bit late and he'd probably just get an earful.

Just at that moment a middle-aged bloke came staggering around the corner and made for the doorway. He gave Tugs a funny look as he passed but seemed more intent on remembering the code for the entrance. He found the right numbers on the keypad and stumbled through the door, muttering something to himself. Just before it clicked shut, Tugs put his hand out and stopped it. The bloke was too intent on catching the lift and didn't look back.

Tugs held the door slightly open, waiting until the lift had come and gone, then quietly went inside. He knew which flat to look for. Getting that information hadn't been difficult.

*

They heard a soft knock at the door and shot up simultaneously. Henry moved quickly to the hallway, grabbing the gun as he did. He looked in on Paula who was sitting up in bed and motioned for her to stay there and stay quiet.

There was another knock, but Henry waited, halfway down the hallway with his gun pointed at the door.

"Who is it?" he shouted.

There was a loud bang and the lock exploded into the hallway. Henry dived backwards but a few shards of metal and wood caught him in the thigh and sent him reeling. The gun flew out of his hand as he landed on the carpet.

Tugs kicked the door open, pointed the gun and fired at the figure lying on the hallway carpet. The impact pushed the body further away and he heard it groan. He was just about to fire again when he saw the man's face, contorted in pain. Bollocks. It wasn't Harold. It was his fucking brother. Oh well, thought Tugs, he'll do.

Paula rushed into the hallway at the sound of the gunshots. Tugs looked up and pointed the gun towards her before returning his gaze and his aim at Henry. But his momentary pause had cost him. Henry managed to grab his gun and fired up blindly. The bullet caught Tugs just under the ribs. He felt like he'd been smashed by a sledgehammer and fell back into the doorway. His knees were buckling underneath him, just keeping himself upright by holding onto the door frame.

The trigger felt stiff in Henrys weakening hand. He raised himself up a little and fired off another shot, but it hit the wall above the door. Tugs barely registered the second shot, falling forwards onto his knees, then slowly onto his front, blood oozing onto the carpet.

Paula knelt by Henry as he slumped down again, dropping his gun. She couldn't see where the bullet had gone in, as there was blood all over his suit but instinctively knew what she had to do. As she was getting up, out of the corner of her eye she saw the figure by the doorway hauling itself up. She looked across to see the man holding his stomach as blood flowed over his hand. In his other hand was the gun.

She watched as he slowly raised it, barely able to lift his head to see where he was aiming. She didn't know if he was going to hit her, Henry or anything at all. But Paula wasn't going to take that chance. She calmly but quickly picked Henry's gun off the carpet, pointed it at the man and squeezed the trigger.

She didn't see where it hit him, but knew it had. His body flew backwards again against the doorframe, sliding down until he was sitting slumped against it with his head bowed low. Blood was still oozing from his stomach but now also she could see it soaking through his jacket at the top of his shoulder. Paula knew she hadn't killed him, but it had been enough to stop him.

Her hand hurt and she dropped Henry's gun. She felt strangely calm and was about to go and take the gun from this man when she heard Henry calling to her.

“Call the station” Henry gasped. “Lewis. Ask for Lewis.” Then he collapsed onto his back, staring vacantly up at the ceiling. He couldn’t manage any more.

She kneeled over Henry again, holding his head in her lap. There was total silence now. She looked towards the doorway at the light-skinned black man in the black suit, no longer moving towards his gun. She wondered if he was dead.

Henry looked up at her. “Paula” he implored, gasping.

She stumbled into the living room and picked up the phone, shaking a little in the silent aftermath of the chaos. She dialed for an ambulance first, then asked to be put through to Limehouse station. The man who answered said he’d make sure DS Lewis got the message.

By now a small group had gathered in the corridor outside. The door was broken on its hinges, hanging limply open. They looked down at the man slumped just inside the doorway and the scene in the hallway. They were still there when the ambulancemen arrived.

*

DS Lewis arrived just as the two men were being stretchered into separate ambulances. Neither had the blanket pulled right over their head, which was a relief. Another murder was just what he needed. He recognised both men and spoke to the ambulance crew to find out where they were being taken, then ascended to the flat. He pushed his way through the small crowd still gathered in the corridor, but now further down having been ushered away by one of the officers who'd arrived first.

One of those officers sat awkwardly with Paula, not really knowing what to say as the other bagged up the weapons, trying to avoid the blood.

Lewis nodded towards his officers and surveyed the scene in the hallway. It was carnage. Blood soaked the carpet and adorned the walls and door. He motioned for the young officer to move and sat himself down next to Paula, who looked at him as if he'd come from another planet.

"Is there somewhere you can stay tonight Mrs White? Any family or friends?"

She didn't respond. The reality of the situation was starting to hit home. Lewis turned to the young officer. "Take Mrs White to Mr White's parents house. It's just up the road. The address should be around here somewhere."

Lewis looked at Paula. "Have you got the address Mrs White?"

Paula continued to sit and say nothing, so Lewis turned his attention back to the officer. “Have a root around, see if you can find an address book or something. If not, take her down the station.”

Paula pointed towards a sideboard without looking at either of them. The officer nodded towards Lewis, who got up and went back out to the hallway where the other policeman was kneeling awkwardly, trying to wipe some blood from the sleeve of his uniform on the carpet.

“Get up Cooper” said Lewis. “Get someone down here to put new door on and get rid of that fucking lot in the corridor. You stay put and if anyone else comes here, I want to know right away. I want your report on my desk first thing tomorrow and tell your Dawson in there to do the same when he’s taken Mrs White to her mother in laws.”

“Sir”

“You did well tonight. I’ll make sure it’s noted in my report.”

“Sir” he repeated, with a bit more enthusiasm.

When he was back at the car, Lewis radioed through to one of the units on duty and requested they attend the Royal London hospital tomorrow morning to arrest a black man admitted with a couple of bullet wounds, if he was still alive. The charge was attempted murder and the man was called Anthony Barrett. He also ordered a second, white man admitted with a bullet wound should under no circumstances be arrested, as he was to visit tomorrow and would deal with it personally. The message was received and understood. They were good lads.

*

Eddie Fuller was fast becoming a legend in London. One of the best disposal experts around, his talents were used regularly now that wage snatches and armed blags were becoming increasingly difficult. He loved the blags but the risk was getting higher and the rewards lower. There was good money in disposing but it wasn't something required too frequently. He'd probably knock the robberies on the head soon and specialise in hits. He weighed this up while he waited in his car, across the street from Ray Masons flat. He waited and waited but no one had come, and the lights were all off. It was obvious Ray was well away, and it pissed him off. He'd been looking forward to torturing that poof. Making him feel pain like never before. Then eventually, when he couldn't suffer any more, snuffing his shitty little life out.

Eddie earned his reputation as a pure, thoroughbred gangster. It was a life he lived to the full, with the birds, booze and regular trips to Spain to top up his tan. With his chosen job, it was the only way to live as it could all end tomorrow. He was a man without conscience or empathy, not caring or even thinking about those he'd already killed, or the impact of his actions on the families. Eddie wondered sometimes why people cared about anything at all. It was a concept completely alien to him.

He got on well with most of the firm, but they were wary of him. He didn't care about that either. He wasn't really part of the firm in any case, just available to whoever wanted to pay for his services. This time it'd been Kemble who'd paid him well up to now, but he wasn't going to get any compensation for tonight and knew Harold wouldn't want to use him. So, he was going to top somebody before he left town, just to say goodbye and thanks for nothing.

All this fucking waiting about was driving him round the bend, so he turned on the ignition and drove away, looking back towards the flat one more time, just in case, but it wasn't going to happen tonight.

As he drove towards his own place, he contemplated going over to help Tugs but thought better of it. He could arrive at the wrong time and fuck everything up. All good things must come to an end and his time in the smoke was up for now, but he'd be leaving in style.

Stepney, Christmas Day, 1962

The family are crammed into the living room, which has become a dining room for the day. It's cramped but we're having a good time, so no one cares except mum who keeps asking if we're alright and saying sorry to Paula every five minutes.

She's put on a great spread, though it's been a lot easier this year with the money coming in from Henry and me. A great big Turkey and all the trimmings.

Edward's home from leave and everyone's still proud of him. Even David seems to be enjoying himself for a change.

Mum's making a real fuss over Paula and it's getting a bit embarrassing. I thought she'd lose interest after a while, but it's been nearly two years since I introduced them, and it's like the daughter she never had. Throughout dinner Paula keeps looking over at me and smiling. I'm doing the same in return. We're nervous and excited at the same time.

Dad's retired to his chair but there's no chance of him nodding off yet with all this noise from us lot at the table.

"That was lovely mum, you've done yourself proud again" says Edward.

Mum blushes and flusters a bit as she starts collecting up the plates. She must be delighted with how it's gone today.

"Leave the washing up. I'll see to it later" Edward continues. "I'm just off outside for a fag."

He gets up to leave as mum takes the dishes out to the kitchen. I get up and follow him outside.

We're standing on the steep doorstep outside our family home having a smoke and chatting. It's the usual stuff about how he's getting on, how lovely Paula is and how well mum's doing. Edward's just finishing off his cigarette and before he drops it and stubs it out, turns to face me.

"I hear you and Henry are working for the same fella".

"Yeah" I reply. "George Patterson. Just a local businessman".

"I know who George Patterson is." He says, but there's no hint of disapproval in his voice. "Be careful Harold."

I look back at him and smile. "I can look after me'self".

He stubs his cigarette out and blows out the last of the smoke. "We can all look after ourselves pal. One thing I've learned since I went away is that having a gun doesn't make you invincible. Not when the other bloke has one too."

"I don't have a gun though." I laughingly reply.

"You know what I mean Harold" he continues. "You've got people in your life you care about, and who care about you. Just keep them safe and keep yourself safe. That's all I'm saying."

I'm surprised. I thought he'd be having this conversation with Henry. After all, he's the main breadwinner. Still, I'm happy he thinks this highly of me and I don't want any grief on Christmas day, so I just nod my agreement and put out my fag on the doorstep. We're careful to kick the dog-ends away into the street.

Back inside, Henry and Paula are chatting at the table and dad's starting to look like he's going to nod off. Edward joins them, but I wander along the hallway to the kitchen and find mum and David sorting out the crockery and running a sink full of hot water.

"Edward said he'd take care of the dishes mum" I say.

"Edward's off back to the army the day after tomorrow and needs a rest. David's going to help me out with the dishes" she replies.

David says nothing.

I let it drop. I don't give a monkeys who does the dishes as long as I'm not roped in. "Alright mum" I say. "Before you get started can you and David come into the living room?"

"Oh, what now?" she says, but I know I've got her intrigued.

"It won't take a minute."

We shuffle back down the hallway into the living room. I wait until Mum and David have sat down and Dad's woken from his half slumber. I stand at the end of the table, facing them all. Paula's beaming. She knows what's coming.

"Mum. Dad. Everyone."

Fucking Hell I sound like Julius Ceasar. And Henry obviously thinks so too. "Lend me your ears" he says.

We all laugh but I want this to be serious. Done properly. So, I put my hands up to shush them and carry on. "I wanted you all to be the first to know that I've asked Paula to marry me and thank Christ she's agreed. We're going to tie the knot."

Everyone looks across at Paula who's still beaming. It's a commotion but mum is the first across to her of course. My brothers get up and shake my hand. Then mum and dad come over to offer their congratulations. We knew it'd be a nice surprise and a lovely way to end Christmas dinner. We also knew mum would be delighted to be told before Paula's parents. I can't see that going so quite so well.

Sunday 9th March 1969

As the sun rose over the capital, Harold sat in silence in a private room of the Royal London Hospital with his wife, his parents and Detective Sergeant Dave Lewis. Laying in the bed before them all was Henry White, severely wounded but clinging to life.

Harold felt accusing eyes on him. Part of him wanted to deny his culpability. Henry was just as involved in this game and they all knew it. But there was another part that accepted his role. Being in charge was having people look to you when things went wrong, getting angry and frustrated when they realise you don't have all the answers and can't perform miracles.

One pair of eyes in that room looked at him without accusation, but keen interest. They belonged to Lewis, who was clearly itching for a word alone. Eventually Harold motioned over to him with a slight incline of his head and they left the room together, both glad to be away from it all for a while.

As they walked together along the corridor, Harold exhaled loudly.

"He's going to be alright Harold" said Lewis. "The bullet didn't hit anything vital, so he should be out in a few weeks. He was lucky though. Another inch to the left..."

They left that thought where it was.

"It hit my brother. That's vital in my book. Anyway, what's going on with Tugs?" Harold enquired.

"He's in bad shape but he'll probably live. We've nicked him for attempted murder. I've put my neck on the block about Henry having a gun, but top brass will be a lot more accommodating if this puts an end to things. I need this to be over now Harold".

He knew what Lewis was angling for. The 'good boy, well done' routine and a few quid. Mind you, he had to admit Lewis had earned his corn. He could have been sitting in a police cell now along with half of his firm. Harold decided to give him what he wanted.

"You can let them know it's over. I have it on good authority the rest of the Wapping firm will come over without fuss, and Fuller's had it away on his toes. You've done well for me and I won't forget it. I'll have a word with Jack later and he'll put you on the payroll. You've earned it."

It sounded a bit patronising but Lewis swallowed it. An arrangement like this could be very lucrative so he wasn't going to bite the hand that fed him. This was his real opportunity, not the promotion which would bring a little more money and a lot more grief.

"I'd better get back" said Harold. "You know how it is". It was a dismissal.

"Of course. I'll be seeing you soon then Harold. Stay out of trouble and watch out for the boys in blue." Lewis smiled, then turned and walked away down the corridor, having got exactly what he'd wanted.

Harold went back to the private room. Everyone was sitting exactly as they'd been ten minutes ago when he left, almost as if time had stood still. Henry had been conscious for a short while earlier that morning before Harold arrived. He'd been very weak but found the strength to tell their mother he wanted to make a fresh start in Australia. Although it would mean another of her sons abroad it pleased Gladys. It was better that than visiting him in the cemetery, and she'd always fancied the idea of going to Australia for a few weeks in the sun.

Henry was sleeping now, and it was Arthur who finally broke the long, strained silence. "David's on his way over with his family. They should be here soon. Are you staying Harold?" It was more of a warning than a question.

Harold looked at Paula, then at his father. "We should probably be getting off soon. There's a lot to sort out back at the flat." He looked over again for some sign of recognition from his wife but got nothing.

They waited mostly in silence with the occasional question or comment from his father. His mother and wife remained totally silent and after half an hour of this Harold couldn't stand it any longer. If David turned up and started throwing accusations around that'd tip him over the edge.

He could hear the noise of the hospital outside their door, as the staff went about their business. He wouldn't be able to hear the approach of his youngest brother and his brood, so thought it best he wasn't here when they arrived. He made his excuses and left without really saying goodbye properly to his parents. Paula followed him in silence. As he was leaving the room he looked back at his brother, relieved he'd be alright but realising how close they'd come to losing him. If he really wanted to leave for Australia, then Harold would back him all the way.

They drove home in silence. Back at the flat there was a policeman outside the replacement door. He recognised them and let them in to get some clothes. As he went into the hallway, Harold saw the dark stains on the hallway carpet. Paula quickly decided she couldn't be in there and went back to wait in the car.

Harold finished packing a suitcase and hung around in the living room for a few minutes. He didn't want to get back in the car a moment before it was necessary, with all those accusations and recriminations simmering just under the surface. As he smoked a fag and stared out of the window, over the Stepney rooftops, he thought about his mother and knew deep down she'd come around, once Henry was safely away and living it up on the other side of the world. What he wasn't so sure about was whether his marriage would survive. By God his mother could hold a grudge, but she had nothing on Paula. She'd been part of the carnage and held it together until she'd got to his mother's house before breaking down. There was pandemonium for a while, with both his wife and mother in bits. The young constable who'd accompanied Paula felt concerned enough to call Lewis, who in turn got a message to Harold via Jack. It had taken several attempts before he woke from his drunken slumber, and even longer for the news to sink in. He got a cab back to his mother's house, not worried now that Tugs was out of the way.

By the time he arrived he'd sobered up completely and just felt empty and exhausted. Eventually, when the shouting and screaming had died down, he did what he knew he needed to do and took control of the situation.

This morning she was calm again, but in a different way. Cold and distant.

Harold also wondered about his own future. Maybe one day he'd end up like Henry, in a hospital bed with tubes sticking out of him and being gawped at by loved ones. Or even murdered by someone he trusted. But you couldn't think that way, or you'd end up going mad.

He finished his fag and stubbed it out in the ashtray on the windowsill, taking a final glance over the familiar rooftops before he headed off for a much-needed break. His gaze would reach new territories now. The cranes in the distance were his, along with a piece of everything they unloaded. It had been five brutal days, but now it was over, and the East End belonged to him.

*

Nurse Renea Bailey emigrated to England from Jamaica over year ago and quickly found herself a job, a dingy flat and on the receiving end of a load of abuse from her neighbours. She was a strong and determined woman, extremely competent in her job. Though she was always polite and kind to everyone she worked with, they knew better than to take liberties. Her firm but fair approach was helping now as she finally ushered out the family of the young man lying in the private room.

The mother had been stubborn, not wanting to leave at first, but after a mixture of gentle and firm persuasion, the lady followed the rest of her family and now, at last she could get on with her job. She cleaned and re-dressed the man's wounds and could tell from his injuries that he wasn't out of the woods yet. She worked methodically and would be late finishing her shift again, but she took pride in her work and did things properly, unlike a lot of them around here. She would do whatever it took to make sure this young man had the best chance possible of recovering and leading his life, even if she had to wait another hour for the next bus. It amazed her that some of her colleagues were more worried about getting to the pub or the pictures, or home for dinner than they were about the patient's welfare.

She looked down on the man in the bed and wondered what had led him to this point, lying here with a bullet wound in his stomach and several smaller wounds to his legs and arms. She shrugged to herself, knowing from experience that life was tough and to get by you sometimes needed to make difficult choices. Whatever choices this young man had made had led him to this conclusion. She hoped, if he pulled through, that he'd make better ones.

Nurse Bailey gathered up the old dressing and dumped it in the bin for the porter to collect later, then washed down all the instruments by the bedside and finally straightened the sheets around him. If he was conscious of any of this he wasn't letting on, but she doubted he would be. The painkillers they'd given him would have knocked out an elephant. Now her duties were over, her thoughts turned to what to do for her dinner.

As she left the room, she switched off the lights and the man remained illuminated by the late afternoon sun creeping in through the gap in the curtains. It was a calm scene and the gentle noise from the machinery by his bedside was strangely comforting. She turned away and closed the door, heading down the corridor towards the staff room.

*

Eddie Fuller had been very patient. He'd watched from a safe distance across the car park as Harold and his wife walked to their car from the hospital, saying nothing to each other. He weighed up whether to do them both here and now, but it was too open and there were too many witnesses. When they'd driven away, he made his way inside and then had to wait bloody ages for the rest of the family to leave.

Now, finally, that fucking nurse was on her way. He watched her walk purposely down the corridor from where he'd been sitting. It had been a pain in the arse moving around different waiting rooms and corridors all day long, trying to blend in when he knew everyone looked at him with immediate suspicion. With a face like his it was hardly surprising. If he decided to stare back, they didn't usually hold their gaze for very long.

He'd even gone to get a bacon sandwich at one point. It killed about half an hour and wasn't worth the money.

Now he was getting edgy. If anybody thought he was hanging about deliberately he'd have to move on. It'd be another wasted trip and he'd had enough of those recently. But thank Christ the nurse was finally out of the room. He couldn't believe there was no Old Bill standing guard. How could they have not put a watch on the poor bastard? They must have thought it was all settled, and he wasn't going to complain about that. It was about time he had a bit of good fortune.

Eddie took a final look up and down the corridor. Most of the visitors had left and it was quiet now, apart from the echoes of footsteps and work going on in other rooms. He wandered towards the door and turned the handle. There was a gentle click and he opened it a fraction. Henry White lay there clinging on to life, though not for much longer thought Eddie.

He slipped quietly in, gently closing the door behind him. Henry was blissfully unaware, so he had plenty of time, unless that nurse or someone else came around. But things were winding down for the evening, so he doubted she'd be back any time soon.

He had to make a proper job of it. He wanted to let Harold White know this was deliberate and not just a machine failure or Henry giving up on life. He toyed with the idea of removing some of the tubes but that would just send the staff running when the alarms went off. And it wouldn't have the personal touch which was much more Eddie's style.

The switchblade opened with a satisfying click. He moved round the side of the bed and looked down at the poor sod. Eddie had been waiting for a chance like this for the past few days and he was going to enjoy it, even if it was as easy as shooting fish in a barrel. He lined the knife up, pointed just underneath the kidney and pushed hard. Then several things happened at once.

There was a short exhalation of air from the mouth and wound, the body arched and the tone on the machine went up quite a few notches. It turned from an intermittent beep to a continuous screech. A gurgling sound coming from the mouth of Henry White as he struggled, but it was short and fruitless. In his weakened state, what remained of his life quickly left his body and the tone on the machine was now a low, continuous noise.

He quickly wiped the blood off the blade onto the bedsheets and slipped out of the room, having witnessed the inevitable. Henry White was dead and the act of plunging the knife in had brought Eddie enough satisfaction.

He was virtually at the end of the corridor when he heard the echoed pounding of shoes running on the tiled floor, getting closer to the room. He fought the urge to turn around. It wouldn't do any good and one of them might get a look at his face, so he walked quickly down the stairs but didn't run. In no time he was out and across the car park, hopping over the low wooden fence and wandering up the road to his car. Before he got in, he took a last look back at the hospital. Outwardly it showed no signs of the panic now ensuing on one of its wards.

As he drove out of the city towards the countryside, Eddie mulled over his plans. He'd had plenty of time to think about things and decided a short trip to Cornwall would be just the ticket. Harold's lot would know straight away that he was responsible, and the police would be out looking too, but they wouldn't know about his family ties in that part of the world and even if they found out, he'd have moved on long before they could track him down. He'd picked up enough cash to last him a good few weeks then he'd disappear up to the North or maybe even further afield. There would always be work for a man like him, and one day it might even be safe enough to return to the smoke. For the time being though, he'd be well out of it and would just have to imagine the Hell that was breaking loose for Harold White. The thought of it made him smile.

*

She'd not spoken to him in the flat or in the taxi. But now they were here, in the plush surroundings of one of the best Mayfair Hotels she was beginning to ease off. The icy wall of silence was slowly defrosting, partly because of the passage of time, partly out of necessity and partly due to their current surroundings that hinted of a lifestyle to come.

Paula unpacked whilst Harold lay on the bed staring out of the huge glass French windows, across at the building over the road.

"What side of the bed do you want?" she asked him.

He smiled briefly. As if he really had a choice. She always slept nearest the window.

"Nearest the door. Listen love..." he started but was interrupted.

"Don't Harold. I don't want to talk about it. Because talking about it makes me think about it and I'm trying to get it out of my mind, though God knows it's been bloody impossible so far. Please don't make it worse."

Harold understood. There were things he wanted to forget, to drive out of his mind forever. But he couldn't. Not yet at any rate. In time, the memories would fade, and life would move on, but it was going to take them both a while to get over the past few days.

Paula went back to unpacking their clothes. As she hung them in the wardrobe, she thought about telling Harold she didn't blame him for what had happened just to make things a bit easier for them both. Is that what good gangster's wives did? Well bollocks if that was going to be her. She may be the wife of a gang boss now, but she was going to remain her own woman, and if she blamed him for something, he was going to know about it. She wasn't going to bow down to him or make his life any easier than it should be, just to keep him happy.

Harold, on the other hand, didn't really care whether she blamed him or not. He'd felt confident that a few days away, a bit of shopping and some decent food would do them good. They'd go back to Stepney, but to a new place, bigger and better than the one they had. They couldn't live in the flat now, not after what had happened there. Until then they'd have a taste of the good life, and that'd go a long way towards changing how she felt about him. The lazy smile he'd been wearing for the past few minutes turned to a frown at the thought of having to see his mother again. He didn't even want to think about how he was going to approach that one. Maybe he could get Paula onside enough over the next few days and she could come with him to work her magic on the old lady.

He also had some big ideas about his firm and now he had the chance to put them into action. He was going to grasp this opportunity with both hands. He had the docks and everything that came along with them. The clubs and casinos here in the West End would come later, but it wouldn't do any harm to sample a bit of what they had to offer in the meantime. He knew he'd be recognised and made welcome, enjoying the trappings of his new status. The smile came back to his face. He was the guv'nor.

The phone on the dresser started to ring. Surely not already, though Harold. He'd left strict instruction that he wasn't to be disturbed except in a genuine emergency. He sighed to himself as he got off the bed and made his way across to answer it. Some of those clowns needed to ask his permission to tie their own shoelaces.

He picked up the receiver. It was reception asking if he'd take a call from a "Gentleman called Jack. Wouldn't give his surname, Sir." Harold agreed, and the Jack he was expecting came on the line.

Harold stood in silence as Jack spoke. Paula watched from the other side of the room as his body sagged and head dropped. She continued watching as he said "Alright", placed the receiver gently back on its cradle and just stood there, resting his hands on the edge of the dresser and looking down.

After about thirty seconds of silence, Paula was just about to go to him, to ask what the phone call had been about. But before she did, Harold White let out a cry of rage and punched the glass mirror on top of the dresser, leaving it smashed and bloodstained as he sank down onto his knees and put his head into his bloodied hands.

Paula heard him. The words were muffled and thick with tears, but she heard "they've killed him" and she knew it was Henry he was talking about. She also knew there would never again be any kind of normality in their lives. This was the price and it wasn't one she was prepared to pay any more. Despite the voice inside her that told her to go to him, hold and comfort him, she walked out of the room, out of the hotel and into the quiet West End streets.

Stepney, 1969

It's been raining, and there's a light mist in the air. You can smell the freshly cut grass.

I'm standing here in a brand new, hand-made black suit and overcoat, while they lower my brothers' body into the ground. It's a large turnout with all the chaps here to pay their respects, even some from Limehouse. Ray isn't here, for obvious reasons. It's probably safe for him to come back now but I want to be certain. In any case, I don't think Henry would've been all that upset that by Ray's absence.

Mother is under an umbrella, crying and leaning on Edward who's been given compassionate leave to attend. Dad stands alone looking like he'd rather be anywhere else in the world. It's cut him up just as bad as mum, but he deals with it in a different way. Edward looks across at me and I can tell he understands.

The vicar finishes saying his word's but no one's really listening. He makes the sign of the cross and turns to leave. The gravediggers are hanging around but at a fair distance, being extra respectful as they know who Henry was, and who I am.

We stand there for a while, paying our final, silent respects. Eventually mum turns to leave, pulling Edward along with her. David and his wife are next to move off, and the rest take that as the sign to start shuffling away. Paula, who's been holding onto my arm, but only for effect, pulls free and walks off, trying to catch up with mum. I'm left standing alone, looking at the open grave and down at the coffin holding the body of my brother. I don't feel responsible. I don't feel guilty. This was the life Henry chose. He wouldn't have blamed me, and that's all that matters.

The anger comes in waves. It was totally unnecessary and out of order. The war was over and no one else needed to suffer. It was just petty revenge and if what I'm hearing is true, Eddie Fuller carried it out off his own back, just to satisfy his sick desires. There's no point in looking for him though, he'll be well gone by now. Something will turn up eventually. Someone will know where's he's ended up and word will reach my ears. I don't care if it takes twenty years, I'll fucking well finish him.

But I'm angry with myself as well. I should have left someone with him but didn't think for one second that anything like this would happen. I've learned a very valuable and costly lesson. I've changed as a result, and people are starting to notice. The East End belongs to me and I intend to do whatever it takes to keep it. I'm going to make sure no one ever hurts me or mine ever again.

As for me and Paula, who knows where that's heading. She hasn't been the same since things kicked off and I can't say I blame her. Nothing has been the same and I think deep down she was happy with the life we had. I can't go back and change the things I've done. They had to be done. Once the twins were inside someone had to step up and take control. If it hadn't been me, then it would have been Kemble, and I'd have been stuck as a driver or messenger boy for the rest of my life, if I'd had any part to play at all. Most likely I'd have ended up at the bottom of the Thames.

I can hear the gravediggers as they lean on their spades, smoking and chatting. Neither of them wanting to look over in this direction in case they catch my eye. But I've no problem with them, they're only wanting to get on and do their job. So, I let them. I turn and walk away, down the sloping graveyard back towards the church and waiting cars. Some have already left for the wake, which has been organised by others and paid for out of my pocket, along with everything else today. Not that it makes a blind bit of difference to some people. David's in the car but Edward is waiting outside, finishing a fag. I think he wants to speak to me, and I could really do with a cigarette and a few words with him, but they all want to get going so I just motion for Edward to get into the car and I climb into the passenger seat. It'll have to wait until later.

The End

20667117R00116

Printed in Great Britain
by Amazon